"*This is Val, our son.*"

Zoë saw no point in softening the blow. When had Justin ever considered her?

"I only have your word for that. What kind of an idiot do you take me for, Zoë? Discovered how wealthy I am now, is that it?"

She stared up at him through a mist of pain and rising anger that she did not attempt to hide.

"No, it's not your money I need, it's you."

JACQUELINE BAIRD began writing as a hobby when her family objected to the smell of her oil painting, and immediately became hooked on the romantic genre. She loves traveling, and worked her way around the world, from Europe to the Americas and Australia, returning to marry her childhood sweetheart. She now lives in the northeast of England and has two grown-up sons. She enjoys playing badminton and spends most weekends with husband Jim, sailing their Gp. 14.

Books by Jacqueline Baird

HARLEQUIN PRESENTS
1558—DISHONOURABLE PROPOSAL
1683—MASTER OF PASSION
1726—GAMBLE ON PASSION

Don't miss any of our special offers. Write to us at the following address for information on our newest releases.

Harlequin Reader Service
U.S.: 3010 Walden Ave., P.O. Box 1325, Buffalo, NY 14269
Canadian: P.O. Box 609, Fort Erie, Ont. L2A 5X3

JACQUELINE BAIRD

The Valentine Child

Harlequin Books

TORONTO • NEW YORK • LONDON
AMSTERDAM • PARIS • SYDNEY • HAMBURG
STOCKHOLM • ATHENS • TOKYO • MILAN
MADRID • WARSAW • BUDAPEST • AUCKLAND

ISBN 0-373-11795-7

THE VALENTINE CHILD

First North American Publication 1996.

Copyright © 1995 by Jacqueline Baird.

Printed in U.S.A.

CHAPTER ONE

His lips were warm on the tender skin of her throat. Somewhere along the way Nigel had removed his T-shirt and she could feel the heat of his body through her fine silk blouse. She closed her eyes tight and told herself that she was enjoying his kisses. It was Nigel—her friend, her colleague and soon to be her lover.

They were sprawled across the sofa in Zoë's London apartment, the only sound Nigel's heavy breathing. She felt his fingers at the buttons of her blouse and tensed, then forced herself to relax. Hadn't she planned this? She was twenty, and still a virgin! And now she was finally going to be a woman! So why did she feel sick?

The thought stopped her cold, and, shoving at Nigel's chest, she said, 'No, Nigel. Get off.' The ensuing tussle was undignified and bordering on the ridiculous. Zoë struggled from beneath his sprawling body but her elbow caught him in the eye, and his yelp of pain was drowned out by the ringing of the doorbell, followed by loud and rapid knocking.

'Saved by the bell!' Zoë murmured, and dashed across the room. Whoever was calling after midnight was in danger of waking the whole house. Her apartment was one of six in a converted Victorian town house.

She flung open the door, about to demand what all the urgency was for, and stopped. Her mouth fell open and she brushed a small hand through the tumbled mass of her silver-blonde hair, sweeping it out of her eyes to get a better view. It couldn't be... But it was... Justin Gifford.

For a second she saw the old Justin, as he had been before the fatal night of her eighteenth birthday. He was smiling tenderly down at her, his dark eyes filled with some emotion she could not guess at.

'Justin.' She said his name, and raised her hand as though to touch him, but he brushed past her and into the room. She closed the door and turned around. Obviously she had been mistaken about his tender glance, she thought dryly.

'So that's what stopped you.' Nigel's voice broke the tense silence. 'You heard the bell.'

Zoë glanced at Nigel, who was sitting on the sofa, struggling to pull his shirt back on, and then back at Justin.

The comparison was inevitable. Nigel looked like a flushed, frustrated twenty-one-year-old—which he was. Whereas Justin, at thirty-five, and touching six feet tall, exuded an aura of sophisticated, arrogant masculinity that was undeniable. Certain of his place and power in the world as a top barrister with a glittering future, tipped to be one of the youngest judges ever appointed, he dominated those around him without even trying.

He was doing it now! Standing in the centre of the room, a long cashmere overcoat draped casually over his broad shoulders. Beneath it a black wool roll-neck sweater moulded the muscular contours of his broad chest, and black denim jeans did the same for his long legs. His night-black hair was, unusually for him, rumpled in disarray and the contempt in his eyes, as he recognised at a glance what had been going on, was unmistakable.

His gaze swept over her small, dishevelled form and the furious glitter in his deep brown eyes would have made a saint quake...

'Does your lover live with you?' he demanded harshly.

Zoë tensed, and wiped her damp palms nervously down her jean-clad thighs. She wriggled her bare toes in the deep-pile carpet and straightened her shoulders in a vain attempt to add inches to her diminutive stature. She tilted back her head and looked a long way up into angry eyes.

'I don't think that is any of your business, Justin. More to the point, what are you doing here at this hour?' She was proud—her voice sounded firm when inside she was trembling. Nigel was not helping any by pulling his shirt down with one hand and knuckling his eye with the other, looking like a drowsy, sated male.

'I'm making it my business, Zoë.' Justin stepped towards her, his massive frame looming over her. She had nowhere to go; her back was at the door. 'Is that the kind of pipsqueak you prefer?' he demanded scathingly. 'I can't say I admire your taste. Get rid of him. Now.'

'Nigel is my guest——' she spluttered.

'So he doesn't live here?' Justin cut in, and simply grabbed her arm and swung her behind him while roaring at Nigel, 'You—whatever your name is—get out.'

Nigel got to his feet. 'Wait just a minute. Who the hell do you think you are? Zoë and I——'

'There is no Zoë, not for you. Now out, before I throw you out.'

Zoë had seen Justin angry before, but never like this. 'You'd better go, Nigel,' she said quietly. Justin's hand around her wrist relaxed slightly at her surrender to his request . . .

'It's OK. Justin is my uncle's partner; I'll be all right,' she assured him, and she was free. Involuntarily she rubbed her wrist as she stepped away from Justin's towering presence, looking, if she did but know it, as if she was wringing her hands in agitation.

After a token objection Nigel left, and Zoë didn't blame him. She had first met Justin Gifford as a sad and frightened fourteen-year-old who had just lost her actor parents in an air disaster in California. She had been swept from her boarding-school in Portland, Maine, to be deposited on her only relative, Uncle Bertie Brown, in England.

She remembered as if it were yesterday. Born and brought up in the States, with an American mother and an English father, she had arrived in what to her had been an alien country, to live in a huge old house, "Black Gables", with an uncle she had never met before.

She had been curled up on the window-seat in the garden-room, quietly crying, when a deep voice had said softly, 'Are you all right, little girl?' She had looked up into the darkest brown eyes she had ever seen, set in the tanned, attractive face of Justin Gifford. Tall and built like a quarter-back, with the broken nose to prove it, he had swung her on to his lap and comforted her and she had been smitten with her first ever crush on a member of the opposite sex.

She glanced warily at him; he was positively bristling with rage and Justin in this mood was dangerous. The only other time she had seen him as mad had been the terrible night of her eighteenth birthday party. Justin had arrived at the party with a red-haired woman in tow—Janet Ord—and Zoë had been consumed by jealousy.

Ever since moving in with her uncle and first seeing Justin she had adored him, even though at twenty-eight he'd been twice her age. Justin had spent many a weekend at the house in Surrey and had always treated Zoë with the greatest kindness. They had talked, laughed and played tennis together.

Every year a valentine card had arrived at Black Gables for her with the simple message "Thinking of you, from your tall, dark, handsome friend". The postmark had been from London and, as Justin was the only man she'd known in the city, she had hoarded the cards as tokens

of his love. In her girlish heart she'd honestly believed
that he loved her as she loved him.

Her birthday party had changed all that. Furious that
he had brought a woman with him, Zoë had stayed up
until four in the morning waiting for Justin to return
from driving Janet home, and then had tried to seduce
him.

A grim smile twisted her full lips at the memory. It
hadn't worked. Justin had taken one penetrating look
at her, dressed in only a flimsy nightie, and had laughed
out loud.

'Run along to bed, little girl, before you get more than
you bargained for,' he had drawled with mocking
amusement.

Instead she had thrown her arms around his neck and
pressed her slender body against him, and demanded that
he kiss her. She had known he wanted to... What followed was engraved in her mind forever.

'Maybe I will at that,' he had growled as his strong
arms had closed around her. His dark head had swooped
down, and he'd proceeded to ravage her mouth with
hard, passionate kisses.

At first she'd exulted in his fierce passion but he'd
made no concession to her youth or innocence and when
his large, strong hands had swept all over her trembling
body, and she'd felt the full force of his masculine ag-
gression, she'd been suddenly terrified by the savagery
she had unleashed and had cried for him to stop.

They had not been friends since. Zoë made a point
of not being at Black Gables when she knew Justin was
arriving for the weekend. It hadn't been difficult—what
with studying at art college and moving to her own
apartment, she had rarely seen him over the past couple
of years.

'Fasten your blouse, for God's sake!' A deep, grating
voice broke into her troubled reminiscences.

'What...?' She glanced down at herself, and felt a tell-tale tide of colour flood her pale face. 'Oh!' she gasped. Her blouse was open to the waist, revealing her firm, high breasts hardly covered by a wisp of white lace. Head bent, with trembling fingers she fastened her blouse. She might not have seen Justin for ages, but she was horrified to realise that he still had the power to make her blush like a lovesick schoolgirl.

Taking a deep breath, she bravely raised her head, her blue eyes clashing with furious brown ones. 'Is it possible you have some explanation for bursting into my apartment in the middle of the night? Or perhaps you've been drinking?' she prompted with all the hauteur she could muster.

In the blink of an eye a shutter seemed to fall over his hard face, masking all expression. 'Sorry, Zoë, you're right of course. You're a grown woman; your private life is none of my business.'

'Big of you to recognise that,' she drawled sarcastically.

'Cut the sarcasm and sit down. I have some bad news.'

'News?' And suddenly she was filled with a dreadful foreboding. She should have realised immediately that nothing short of a major catastrophe would have bought Justin to her apartment in the middle of the night.

She moved towards him; her small hand clasped his forearm. 'What has happened?' Her beautiful face paled; her eyes searched his rugged features. 'Not...?'

'There's no easy way to say this. Bertie has had a massive heart attack and is in Intensive Care at the local hospital. I'll take you to him.'

'Will he be OK, Justin?' Zoë asked the question for the hundredth time of the brooding figure sitting beside her on the banquette in the cold waiting-room of the hospital.

He turned his dark head, compassion in his steady gaze. 'Of course he will be, little one. Your uncle Bertie is a fighter.' And, curving a long arm around her slender shoulders, he drew her into his side. 'Snuggle up and try to rest, hmm?' With his other hand he brushed the tumble of blonde hair from her brow. 'I'll look after you; after all, that's what friends are for.' He smiled softly, giving her shoulder a brief squeeze.

Comforted by his reassuring words and held against the warmth of his hard body, she forgot the humiliation, the embarrassment that had made her avoid him for the past two years. Instead she lifted her sapphire-blue eyes to his harshly handsome face and said, 'Are we friends again?' And they were.

Two weeks later, when Bertie was released from hospital a month before Christmas, Zoë willingly gave up her apartment and returned with her uncle to Black Gables, quite happy to commute every day to her job as a graphic artist at Magnum Advertising in London if it meant spending her free time with her uncle.

Zoë positively danced into the breakfast-room. 'Good morning, Uncle Bertie.' She pressed a swift kiss on the parchment-like cheek of the old man sitting at the pine table. 'You're looking better today,' she said, with a quick smile, though in reality she was worried about him. His once tall, raw-boned figure seemed to be shrinking by the day. His fine head of silver hair appeared lank and somehow lifeless. But she did not betray her worry as she asked, 'Any post for me today?'

'Yes, two, minx.' He smiled fondly back at her. 'And thank you.' He waved a card, with a big red rabbit sitting in a heart on the front, in her face. 'It was kind of you to think of me.'

Chuckling, she took the two envelopes he held out to her and, plonking down on the nearest chair, ripped them open. One was obviously from Bertie. 'You're not supposed to sign them, you know, Uncle,' she admonished, and then went dreamy-eyed over the next valentine card: 'Thinking of you, from your tall, dark, handsome friend.'

She just knew it was Justin and tonight she was going to tell him she had known all along. Finally she was confident enough in herself and her new-found adult relationship with him.

Over the past months he had been a tower of strength, visiting most weekends, and the rapport he shared with Uncle Bertie had naturally spread to include her again. They had shared the occasional dinner date; Justin had taken her to the theatre, and the ballet and, most important of all, at the end of their evenings out he had always kissed her goodnight, and always left Zoë aching for something more. But tonight Justin was taking her to the Law Society's Valentine's Ball at a top London hotel, and she just knew that tonight would be special.

'Not going to work today, young lady?' Uncle Bertie's question broke into her happy reverie.

'No, I have the day off, and I'm going to pamper myself shamelessly because Justin's taking me to the ball.'

'I see . . .' His watery blue eyes crinkled at the corners. 'Good. He's a fine young man. You couldn't do better.'

'I know,' she agreed, with a cheeky grin.

A dozen hours later Zoë heard Justin arrive as she blotted her lipstick for the final time. She seldom bothered much with make-up, having a fine clear skin, but tonight she had gone to town and she was delighted with the result.

Her eyes were huge, her brows and lashes subtly darkened, and a faint touch of colour on her eyelids served to enhance the sparkling blue of her eyes. She had used a light foundation that seemed to make her skin gleam almost translucently. And, daringly, she had coloured her wide, full-lipped mouth in a bright cerise lip-gloss that exactly matched her gown.

The dress was a romantic dream, she thought happily, floating out of her room and down the grand staircase to where Justin and her uncle waited. Designed in cerise satin, demure cap sleeves set off the plunging, heart-shaped, fitted bodice that nipped her waist and ended in black embroidered points over her hips, then flared out into a wide skirt with an underskirt of frothy layers of black net.

The assistant in Harvey Nichols had assured her that the nineteenth-century romantic look was all the rage and, when she stopped halfway down the stairs to glance down at Justin, and saw the flare of admiration in his eyes, she knew she had made the right choice.

Justin—tall, dark and incredibly impressive in a conservative black dinner-suit—moved to the stairs and held out his hand to her. She felt like a princess as he led her down the last few steps.

'You have grown into an amazingly beautiful woman, Zoë. You look absolutely stunning.' His dark eyes gleamed with admiration and some other emotion that Zoë hoped was love.

'Thank you, kind sir,' she said prettily.

A wry smile curved Justin's firm mouth. 'But I knew I should have asked. I'm no good at all at this romance thing.' And, handing her a clear cellophane box, with a shrug of his broad shoulders he added, 'For you. And before you say anything even I know a corsage of red roses will clash with your dress. Sorry...'

'I love them, but you shouldn't have; your valentine card has always been enough for me,' she declared openly, her eyes sparkling with happiness. 'Wait till I get my cape; the corsage will look great on it.'

Dashing back upstairs, she didn't see Justin's dark scowl or hear his muttered, 'What card?'

'Right, I'm ready.' She returned, holding out her velvet cloak for Justin to place around her shoulders. She shivered with delicious anticipation when his strong fingers caressed her flesh as he fastened the cap and solemnly pinned the red roses on the velvet above her breast.

With Uncle Bertie's good wishes, and his admonition to stay in town for the night ringing in her ears, Justin led her out to the car—a sleek black BMW—and slid in beside her.

Justin was the perfect partner; he insisted on dancing every dance with her, and the evening took on a magic all of its own. She could not help but observe the respect and esteem he attracted from his fellow professionals. She overheard in the powder-room that it was rumoured that he was definitely going to be on the next list of judges, and, on returning to the ballroom, she could not resist teasing him unmercifully.

'Such exalted company. Why, m'lud, I fear you give me the vapours.' She fluttered her thick lashes unashamedly.

'I'd like to give you a lot more,' he drawled mockingly, his brown eyes smiling down into hers. 'You little tease.'

'Who—*moi*? Your honour! No, your honour!' She camped it up, pressing a hand to her heart.

'You're asking for trouble, little one,' Justin opined, and swept her into his arms and on to the dance-floor.

'If... or... when...' he spaced the words out as they moved slowly and lazily around the floor to the haunting strains of 'Unchained Melody' '...I...am...made... a...judge...' he curled her small hand in his and held it against his chest while his other hand stroked up her back to bury beneath the silken fall of her pale blonde hair and curve around her nape '...it won't be "Unchained Melody" we dance to, my love.'

He tilted her face up to his and murmured against her ear, 'I'll sentence you to be chained to me for life.' And then his mouth moved over hers in a kiss as light as the brush of a butterfly's wing.

She clung to him, her eyes shining like stars; her breasts, hard against his chest, throbbed with burgeoning arousal while her heart drummed to an erratic beat. 'If only,' she breathed, licking her suddenly too dry lips.

His dark eyes followed the movement of her tongue. 'Not if—when,' he rasped, his arms tightening around her until even through the many layers of her gown Zoë could feel his hardening need, and she finally admitted to herself that nothing had changed—her schoolgirl crush had turned into a woman's love for a man.

'Let's get out of here,' he said urgently.

'But it's only eleven.'

'The way I feel right now, I won't live to midnight.' Their eyes met and clung—no more teasing, no amusement, just a basic primeval need.

'Yes,' she agreed softly.

Back in Justin's apartment, she barely noticed the décor; she had eyes only for Justin.

He stripped off her velvet evening cloak and dropped it to the floor, then, catching her hand, hurried her down a hall through a door and into a large room—his bedroom! She hesitated, eyeing the king-size bed warily. Was she ready for this? But the question was answered by Justin.

'Zoë.' He cupped her small face in his large hands and tilted her head back, his deep brown eyes darkened to almost black. 'Don't be afraid. You know I would never do anything to hurt you. But I feel as though I've waited aeons for you. I can't wait any longer.' His mouth brushed gently over hers. 'I promised myself I would do this properly,' he breathed against her lips.

She reached her slender arms around his neck, her heart melting with love, and felt anything but proper... She gazed up into his dark eyes, and was surprised to see a hint of uncertainty, a touching vulnerability in their black depths. 'Do what?' she encouraged with a dreamy smile.

His hands lowered, one to curve around her waist, the other to go to his jacket pocket. 'Ask you to be my valentine tonight and always. Be my wife,' he husked, and, putting a little space between them, he showed her the velvet ring-box.

Zoë, her eyes misted with tears of joy, took the box and opened it. A gasp of delight escaped her at the sight of the diamond and sapphire ring. 'Put it on for me.' She held it out with a hand that trembled.

Justin slipped the ring on the appropriate finger. 'I take it that's a yes?' he queried huskily before he enfolded her once more in his arms; his dark head bent and he kissed her, long and tenderly.

She parted her lips at his urging; his tongue seductively traced the inside of her mouth and she was lost. She would be anything he wanted her to be.

'Now, do I get to unwrap my valentine? You, my heart,' he mouthed against her cheek as he spread small kisses all over her face, her eyelids, the slender arch of her throat, while his hands deftly found the zip of her dress.

It was no good; she could stand it no longer; she had to get away for a while. Her head was pounding, and if she had to listen to one more stilted condolence on the death of her uncle Bertie she would break down completely.

'Are you all right, Zoë?'

She glanced up into concerned deep brown eyes and tried to smile. 'I will be when this is over.' A supporting arm closed around her tiny waist and she relaxed against the hard, muscled, masculine frame of her husband of two months—Justin. She still had to pinch herself sometimes to believe that she and Justin were actually man and wife.

'Zoë.' Justin's voice snapped her back to the present.

She raised misty blue eyes to his. 'I'm OK.'

'You're not,' he contradicted her bluntly. His hand tightened fractionally on her waist. 'Slope off to your secret seat, and I'll make sure you're not disturbed for a while.' His hand moved to her back and turned her to the door. His dark head bent, she felt the feather-light brush of his mouth against the top of her head and she was out in the large oak-panelled hall.

Justin knew her so well, she thought, slipping quickly through the door opposite and making straight for the window-seat. Curled up behind the curtain, she stared out of the window. The clear, bright light of a mid-May day glinted over the long lush green lawns and on down to the river, which wound like a sinuous silver snake along the bottom of the garden.

Too nice a day for a funeral! She sighed deeply, and a tear rolled slowly down the curve of her cheek. Uncle Bertie—dead . . .

She wiped away the moisture with the back of her hand. She couldn't have any tears left. She had done her crying for her uncle over the past few months when it had become obvious that it was simply a matter of time before his ruined heart gave out. The funeral today was the last act for a man who had led an exemplary life. The guests across the hall numbered among some of the greatest names in the land, here to pay their respects.

Uncle Bertie had been an eminent judge destined for one of the highest positions in the English judiciary, until he had suffered his heart attack last November.

Zoë closed her eyes and lay back against the wall, her feet tucked beneath her. She was going to miss him, she knew. But—thank God!—she had Justin; she was not alone, and Uncle Bertie had been delighted when she'd married his protégé. So she at least had the solace of knowing that her uncle's last weeks had been happy.

Smiling softly to herself, she glanced at her sparkling engagement ring and the pale gold band beside it. Then she breathed on the window, misting the glass, and, in a childish gesture, drew a heart with her forefinger and inserted the initials ZG and JG with a rather wobbly arrow, remembering the Valentine's ball.

No girl had ever had a more tender, intoxicating initiation into womanhood. Justin was the perfect lover; slowly and carefully he had kissed and caressed, urged and cajoled her through the intricacies of love, and at the final moment had protected her from any untoward consequences.

The next morning, when he had taken her back to Black Gables, he had formally asked Uncle Bertie for her hand in marriage, informed her arrogantly that as his wife-to-be she no longer needed to work, and, of course, she had agreed. Then, a month later, on the arm of her uncle Bertie, she had walked down the aisle of the village church to wed Justin.

She sighed. Who would have thought that two months later Bertie would be dead? Then she heard the voice of Mrs Sara Blacket, the wife of one of the partners in Justin's law firm, speaking.

'It's a magnificent house. Gifford has done very well for himself, even if he did have to marry the old man's niece to get it.'

Why, the cheeky old bat! Zoë thought, and would have moved, but then she recognised another voice—that of Mary Master, the wife of a High Court judge.

'Oh, I don't think Justin married for any mercenary reason. They make a lovely couple, and it's obvious she adores him.'

'I don't dispute the girl loves him, but my Harold told me he'd heard that Bertie Brown, when he realised he was dying, offered Justin his place as the head of chambers on condition that he married the niece. He wanted her settled before he died.'

'I find that hard to believe. In any case, the other partners would have had some say in the matter,' Mary Master argued.

'Bertie was well liked, and which one of them would refuse a dying man's last wish? As Harold said, the girl is exquisitely beautiful, tiny—like a rare Dresden china doll—but young and hardly a match for an aggressively virile male like Gifford.

'His taste in the past was for large, bosomy ladies more his own age. Remember the Christmas dinner two years ago and Justin's redhead partner? Harold told me they were taking bets on whether her boobs would stay covered through to the sweet course.'

'Oh, really, Sara!' Mary exclaimed. 'That's a bit much, and in any case Justin was not dating Zoë at the time. He was a free agent.'

Zoë cringed behind the curtain, her face flaming; she could not believe what the Blacket woman was saying. Didn't want to.

'Believe me or not, Mary, but I wouldn't mind being a fly on the wall when the will is read. Bertie befriended Justin Gifford when he was a teenager and his father died—apparently they were old friends. I'll bet Gifford gets at least half the old boy's estate, if not more. Hardly fair on Zoë, his only living relative.'

'Surely it's not important? They are married—everything they have is divided equally anyway.'

Zoë heard Mary Master reply. The woman's voice was
fading—they were obviously leaving the room—but Zoë
could not move; she was frozen in shock.

'Exactly my point.' Sara Blacket's piercing voice
echoed in the room as she closed the door. 'Gifford is
a very ambitious man and by doing what the old man
wanted and marrying the American girl he has made
doubly sure of getting control of virtually everything. I
can't see young Zoë being involved in finance at all—
she's the arty type.'

Zoë stared at the heart she had drawn on the glass;
the mist was fading, the shape disappearing—a bad
omen! Don't be stupid! she told herself, and quickly
raised her hand and rubbed the window clean. But she
could not clean the doubt in her mind away so easily.
Could it be true? Had Uncle Bertie insisted that Justin
marry her? No, of course not, her common sense told
her. Justin loved her, didn't he?

She slid off the seat and stood up. She was over-
reacting. Sara Blacket was a nosy, overbearing old gossip
whose husband, as the most senior in chambers, had
wanted to be head himself. Justin had told her as much.
Obviously it was pure sour grapes on Sara's part.

'Zoë? Zoë?' Justin's voice broke into her un-
comfortable thoughts, and, smoothing the plain black
jersey shift down over her hips, she moved towards the
door. It was flung open and Justin walked in, his dark
eyes full of concern.

'Ah! There you are. I saw Mary and Sara leave. I take
it you didn't get the peace you were looking for,' he said
lightly, casually slipping an arm around her shoulders.
'Judge Master is waiting in the study, darling. It's time
to say goodbye to the guests, and then the will will be

read. Are you up to it or would your rather wait? There's no hurry.'

'Why? Because you know what's in it?' The curt words had left her mouth before she could stop them...

'No. No, I don't.' Justin turned her around to face him, his arms encircling her waist, holding her loosely, his dark eyes scrutinising her pale face. 'I was thinking of you; you look tired. It's been a long day.'

Held in his arms, conscious of his warmth and the tender care in his expression, Zoë hated herself for doubting him for a minute, but she could not control her wayward tongue. She loved Justin, and she needed his reassurance.

'You do love me, Justin?' she asked softly, her eyes catching his, a pleading light in their sapphire depths.

'Of course I do, silly girl; I married you, didn't I?' And his dark head lowered, blocking out the light as his mouth moved over hers in an achingly tender kiss.

She moved closer into his embrace and curved her slender arms around his neck; she felt his arms tighten and she opened her mouth, inviting the kiss to deepen. She sighed into his mouth, their breath mingling there, tongues entwining; she ran her fingers through his thick black hair, her heart pounding. Justin loved her; he was her husband, her love, her life.

Justin slightly parted his long legs, one strong hand curving down over her bottom and urging her between his muscular thighs. She curved into the hot, hard warmth of his body, her breasts flattened against his ribcage, her nipples tingling with the contact then hardening as his other hand swept up to cup possessively over one high, firm breast through the soft wool of her dress.

He broke the kiss long enough to nuzzle her throat, his mouth covering the madly beating pulse in her neck then trailing back to her softly parted lips; a low moan escaped her just as his mouth found hers once more.

As always she trembled, melting against him, her blood pounding through her veins, but suddenly he was easing her away. 'Justin,' she murmured.

'Easy, Zoë. Now is not the time.'

She raised passion-hazed eyes to his rugged face; she recognised the dark blush of desire staining his taut features at the same time as she saw the familiar iron control reassert itself in the black depths of his eyes.

'You're right, as usual,' she agreed, and was swept into a gentle hug, his large hand stroking the back of her head as he pressed her to his broad chest, easing the sexual tension surrounding them into something more manageable.

'Come on, Zoë; the quicker we say goodbye to the guests, the sooner we can get this day over with.'

He was right, but sometimes, just sometimes, Zoë wished that he would get swept away by passion. But the great Justin Gifford, renowned for his cool, lethal voice, his absolute control of any jury, never, ever lost control.

Now, where had that unkind thought come from? Zoë mused as she saw the guests depart. Justin was British and restraint was an accepted characteristic of the people, and she should know! On first arriving here, a typical American teenager, she had found it difficult to adjust to the more formal way of life.

Half an hour later she followed Justin into the study and sat down beside him on the black hide sofa. Mrs Crumpet, the housekeeper, Jud, her husband—also the gardener—and John Smith, the chauffeur, plus the two daily women, stood around in a rather embarrassed silence as Judge Master sat down in the chair behind Uncle Bertie's desk.

It soon became apparent that Bertie hadn't changed his will in years. All the staff were left generous amounts of money and there were pensions for Mr and Mrs

Crumpet and the chauffeur. His law books were to go to Justin and the remainder of the estate was left to Zoë, with the proviso that Justin be her guardian until she was twenty-five.

'You—my guardian.' She smiled at Justin. 'It sounds slightly kinky as we're already married.'

Judge Master laughed. 'Bertie made this will when you were sixteen; he did think about changing it, but, as you and Justin married, there was no real point. It's all in the family anyway.'

The staff left the room, and then Judge Master revealed the extent of the estate. It was not a great deal of money but, with the house, a very nice legacy. She felt Justin tense beside her, and she shot him a puzzled look, but he ignored her, his gaze fixed on Judge Master.

'With the house included, if he didn't make prior arrangements, the death duty will be quite considerable.' Justin was all business, and Zoë felt oddly excluded as the two men talked literally over her head.

'Yes, I did warn him,' the judge responded.

'But you know Bertie—he refused to admit he was dying right up until the end.'

'I shouldn't worry about the tax, though. Zoë is twenty-one in a month, when she will obtain control of her trust fund from her parents. I was talking to the lawyer in New York only a few days ago, and, with the reissue of an old film of her father's about dinosaurs, apparently her trust fund is quite healthy.'

'How healthy exactly?' Justin asked quietly.

'Double what Bertie left, so the tax should not be a problem. Mind you, I would advise you to sell this place; it's far too big for this day and age. Maintenance alone was always a drain on Bertie's funds.'

'Do you mind, gentlemen? I *am* sitting here,' Zoë intervened, and wanted to laugh as the two males in the room turned to look at her as though she were some apparition.

Judge Master was the first to recover. 'Yes, of course. It has been a long day; Justin and I can discuss all this in a day or two, and I'd better be making tracks or Mary will not be pleased.'

Zoë smiled; she liked Judge Master and, after the conversation she had overheard earlier, she appreciated his wife, who had defended her against the infamous Sara Blacket.

Justin rose to his feet and walked across to the cabinet in the corner of the oak-panelled study. 'You will join me in a drink, Judge? I need one.' He picked up a bottle of whisky, opened it and poured a large shot into a crystal tumbler before adding, 'How about you, Zoë?'

She looked across at her husband; his back was to her, his shoulders tense, and, as she watched, his dark head tilted back as he lifted the glass to his mouth and drank. It was unusual for Justin to drink spirits—an occasional glass of wine was more his style.

'Zoë.' Justin turned, glass in hand. 'Do you want one?' he asked again, his expression austere.

'No. You and the judge carry on. I'll go and find Mary.'

Ten minutes later, she stood in the entrance hall and thanked Judge Master for all his help, but her glance kept straying to Justin at her side as she said goodbye to the couple. She had the oddest feeling that although he was there he was not really with her.

The door closed behind Judge and Mary Master and she sighed in relief.

'At last it's all over,' she murmured, her eyes seeking her husband's. He had been a tower of strength all through the death, the funeral, everything. She could never have managed without him, and all she wanted now was to feel the comfort of his arms around her.

Dressed in a perfectly tailored dark suit, a stark white shirt and the obligatory black tie, he looked all powerful, virile male, as though nothing could touch him or those he cared for. He was her rock, her comfort and her lover, and she had never needed him more than now. She stepped towards him.

'I have some work to attend to, Zoë; I'll see you at dinner.'

She shot him a pleading if puzzled glance and could have sworn that he was avoiding her eyes. 'Yes, OK.' But she doubted whether he heard her as she was talking to his back.

CHAPTER TWO

ZOË knocked on the heavy oak door, turned the handle, opened it and entered the study. Justin was sitting behind the huge mahogany desk in what used to be Uncle Bertie's chair, his broad shoulders hunched, his head buried in a mass of papers.

He had removed his jacket and tie, and his white shirt was open at the neck, the sleeves rolled back to reveal sinewy forearms sprinkled with a downy covering of dark hair. He looked stern and somehow remote. She moved silently across the room but he sensed her presence, his proud head lifting.

'Yes?' he said distantly.

'It's eight—dinner is ready.' She shook her head in disgust at his vacant look, her long blonde hair floating around her shoulders in a silvery cloud as she moved to his side and leant against his broad shoulder. Placing one slender arm around his other shoulder, she added, 'You work far too hard, Justin, and it has got to stop.' She pressed a swift kiss on the top of his head. 'Come and eat.'

'I have to work hard if I expect to keep my beautiful wife in the manner to which she is accustomed,' he retorted, his sensuous mouth curving in a brief smile, and, getting to his feet, he spanned her tiny waist with his strong hands and swung her high in the air, as one would a child. 'And that's my mission in life.'

She grinned down into his handsome face, thrilled by the compliment. 'Not any more, you don't, if what Judge Master said about my trust fund is correct,' she teased.

Justin looked up at her, all trace of amusement deserting his hard features, and abruptly he lowered her to the ground. 'Yes, of course. Apparently I've married a woman of means,' he drawled, stepping back and rolling down the sleeves of his shirt. 'The tax man will certainly see it that way,' he added with dry sarcasm, hooking his jacket with one hand as he headed for the door, and flinging over his shoulder, 'Let's eat.'

She stared at his retreating back for a moment, hurt by the obvious sarcasm in his tone. Was it possible that Justin was disappointed not to have received more in the will? No, he couldn't be. He was a comfortably wealthy man in his own right.

Later, sitting opposite each other across the small table in the breakfast-room, sharing a simple, almost silent evening meal of beef goulash and rice followed by ice-cream, the thought haunted her, and by the time they were sipping their coffee she could contain herself no longer.

'Justin, are you upset by the will?' She had to ask. Absolute honesty was essential to a good marriage—or so all the books said—and she wanted their marriage to be perfect.

His black head lifted, his eyes capturing hers across the table. 'No, certainly not. But why do you ask?' he demanded, the hard tone of his voice jarring on her sensitive nerves.

'Earlier, in the study, you didn't seem too amused when...'

His mouth compressed. 'Today is hardly a day for amusement; we have just buried your uncle,' he prompted, in a voice he usually used to destroy some unsuspecting witness.

'Please, Justin, you don't have to remind me. I just thought... Well, maybe you felt left out.' How could she tell him of the conversation she had overheard? Her own doubts...?

'No, I assure you,' he said, lowering his voice, 'as far as the will is concerned, it was exactly as it should be. Bertie was my guide and mentor all through my career and before, and I am greatly honoured that he left me his law books.'

Zoë believed him; she knew his sentiment was genuine and she wanted to say so, but, as often happened though she was reluctant to admit it, her brilliantly clever husband left her tongue-tied. She only had to look into his deep brown eyes, or note the curve of his mouth as he spoke, and his effect on her was immediate. After two months of marriage her pulse still raced at the sight of him. Tonight a lock of black hair had fallen over his broad brow and unconsciously she reached across the table and brushed it back with her fingers.

Justin caught her hand in his and pressed a quick kiss to her palm, his glance flashing knowingly to her face. 'You've had a long, hard day, Zoë. Leave the worrying to me and go to bed, hmm? I'll join you later.' He squeezed her hand before letting it go to resume drinking his coffee.

But the mention of bed reminded her of another problem she had. The house! Because of Uncle Bertie's ill health when they had married there had been no honeymoon; Justin had simply moved in with them, here at Black Gables.

It was a massive old house, totally impractical and virtually impossible to heat. It contained fifteen bed-rooms and several reception-rooms, plus a ballroom and a dozen attic rooms. In the extensive grounds were two cottages and a range of outbuildings, some with commercial use but long since left derelict.

Her uncle had insisted on having the master suite decorated for them, but unfortunately for Zoë it was built on the old-fashioned lines of two bedrooms joined by a dressing-room and bathroom. She would have much preferred to share a bed with her husband. Instead, she found that after making love Justin invariably went back to his own room...

'About the house, Justin,' she burst out. 'Judge Master suggested we sell it and I'm inclined to agree.'

She was a thoroughly modern girl, having spent the first fourteen years of her life living at home in California and boarding-school in Maine. She had once before broached the subject of separate rooms to Justin, but he had fobbed her off with, 'Best to leave things as they are. There's no point in upsetting Bertie,' and, as a new bride and still in some awe around her dynamic husband, she had let it go. But now...

'I mean the separa——'

'It's your house—you can do what you like with it, but I had thought you felt something for the old place. Obviously I was wrong.' He rose from the table, threw down his napkin, and turned to leave.

'I simply meant it's far too big for us, and you have to travel to London every day.' She jumped up, hurrying after him. She did love Black Gables but she loved her husband more, and she could not bear him to be angry with her.

"Zoë.' He spun round, his hands falling on her shoulders, gripping them tightly. 'Shut up and go to bed; now is not the time to discuss these things. Neither of us is thinking straight.' He looked down into her flushed, puzzled face and sighed, his gaze moving from her sapphire eyes to the long, soft fall of her silver-blonde hair, and finally settling on her wide, soft mouth.

'Are we having our first fight?' She tried to joke, but could not hide the tremor in her voice. The events of the day were finally getting to her, and her self-control was perilously close to breaking.

'No, no, of course not, little one,' he hastened to re-assure her. 'I'm a bit tense, that's all. It's been a sad and difficult few weeks for both of us.' He lowered his head.

She trembled at the first brush of his lips and all rational thought deserted her, and when Justin carefully turned her around and pointed at the stairs she meekly walked up them.

Slipping out of her clothes, she walked into the dressing-room, and, replacing the black wool dress in the wardrobe continued to their shared bathroom, where she placed her undies in the wash-basket.

She pulled on a shower-cap and stepped into the double shower stall. Turning on the water and adjusting it to a pleasant temperature, she tilted back her head and closed her eyes, welcoming the soothing spray. It had been a long, sorrow-filled day and she was tense and tired. Justin was right as usual. Picking up the soap, she lazily lathered the fragrant cream into her naked body.

Her hands stilled on her small, firm breasts. How much nicer it would be if they were Justin's hands. The sensual thought brought a brief smile to her small face. Justin sharing the shower—dream on! She smiled wryly.

Justin was a magnificent lover, as she had discovered on Valentine's night, but she had also discovered in the weeks before her wedding that he possessed a monu-mental self-control, refusing to make love to her again until they were married, however much she had tried to tempt him.

Then, on her wedding night, he had, with skill and patience and a sensitivity she could only marvel at, turned her into a molten mass of pure sensation, leading her to an ecstatic explosion of the senses and emotions that she had never imagined in her wildest fantasies. Plus, he had repeated the miracle almost every night since.

But he was conservative with a small C. They only ever made love at night—in bed! The shower was certainly not Justin's scene.

A frown marring her smooth brow, Zoë stepped out of the shower and wrapped a large, fluffy towel around her slender form. Why, tonight, did the thought of Justin's restraint worry her? It never had before. Surely she wasn't letting the bitchy Sara Blacket's comments get to her? Justin loved her; he had said so, hadn't he?

Much later she lay naked in her bed, trying to keep her eyes open, waiting for him. It had crossed her mind to go to his bed, but, as a relative novice at lovemaking, she somehow found the thought of taking the initiative with her formidable husband oddly intimidating.

Her eyes flew open as she heard Justin entering his room, then the sound of running water in the bathroom. She pulled herself up the bed, tucking the sheet around under her arms, and switched on the bedside light. She waited until the noise from the bathroom stopped, then called his name. She needed him tonight, even if only to hold her and reassure her that she was not alone. He was all the family she had left; he was her world...

'What is it, Zoë?' Justin demanded, walking into the room, a small towel riding low on his hips his only covering. 'I thought you'd be asleep by now.' He crossed to the bed, to look soberly down at her small frame outlined beneath the covers then up to the pure, pale oval of her lovely face.

Her heart turned over in her breast at the sight of him. His night-black hair, damp from the shower, was swept severely back from his broad forehead, throwing his rugged features into prominent relief. His deep brown eyes, the cast of his high cheekbones and his slightly olive-tinged complexion revealed his father's Spanish ancestry, though he never spoke much about his family. She knew his parents were dead, and he had a stepsister who was living with some tribe of Indians in the rainforest on a four-year anthropology study.

'I was waiting for you,' she told him softly, stretching out a slender hand to touch his forearm, her sapphire eyes roaming over him in undisguised want.

His wide shoulders gleamed like gold satin; a thick mat of hair covered his broad chest, and arrowed down in a fine line past his navel to disappear beneath the towel. His long, muscular legs were planted slightly apart, a lighter dusting of hair shading them darker.

'I thought you were never coming,' she murmured, trailing her hand from his arm to thread her fingers through his curling chest hair.

Justin caught her wrist and, easing her hand back behind her head, lowered his big body down beside her and bent his dark head towards hers. 'Oh, I think I will, and very quickly, my darling girl,' he drawled with mocking amusement, but his eyes flashed for an instant with what, to Zoë, looked suspiciously like anger just before his lips brushed over hers in a kiss as light as thistledown.

'I should go to my own bed and let you rest.' He whispered the words against her mouth.

'No. Please, Justin. Don't leave me alone tonight. I need you.'

'Do you? I wonder if you know what it means to actually need someone. You're so hopelessly young,' he said enigmatically, standing and slipping the damp towel from his hips. She was in no doubt that he would stay— he could not hide his state of arousal from her and did not try to as, with a deft flick of his wrist, he flung the covers back, revealing her naked form to his glittering eyes.

'You were waiting for me,' he husked, his heated gaze sweeping over her from where her long hair trailed across the pillow, lingering on her softly parted lips, then again on the pale, round orbs of her perfect breasts, then moving down to the tiny waist and softly flaring hips, and the soft blonde curls at the juncture of her thighs. 'God, but you're beautiful, Zoë. Perfection in miniature,' he growled.

She could feel her whole body blush but she didn't care; he was her husband. 'Not so much of the miniature,' she teased, and stretched out her arms to him in a female gesture as old as time.

He gave her one long look, his face wearing an oddly restrained expression in the shadowy light. Then he dropped to his knees by the side of the bed.

'Justin?' she queried tentatively. Then his hand circled her ankle and his black head bent and his lips brushed a trail of kisses from her ankle to her knee, then her thigh.

She trembled with exquisite emotion as his other hand stroked slowly up over her flat stomach and higher, to close over one firm breast. He rolled the aching tip between his long fingers with delicate eroticism, and she moaned her delight. She felt like some Eastern slave girl, spread on the bed for her master's delectation, but surprisingly she didn't care...

But soon the hedonistic pleasure was not enough. She wanted to kiss him, touch him, rouse him to the same all-consuming need that engulfed her.

She stretched her hand to his shoulder, her slender fingers clawing his hard flesh. 'Please, Justin.'

But Justin knew exactly what he was doing to her, the burning fire he was igniting in her body, and refused to be rushed. With hands and mouth he kissed and caressed while withholding from her the ability to reciprocate, until she was whimpering, crying out her need...

Then and only then did he rise and, nudging her legs further apart, eased his length between them. As he supported his weight on his elbows either side of her head, his mouth sought hers again. The kiss was a passionate statement, his tongue moving in her mouth, echoing his masculine possession...

Her eyes flew open and she saw his rugged face, the skin flushed and taut across his cheekbones, his lips curled back in a feral grimace as he fought to stay in control. Then he moved deeper and deeper inside her, harder, faster, and her eyes closed again as every part of her clenched around him then exploded in a surging tide of shattering pleasure. She felt his great frame shudder and the fierce, pulsing heat of him filled her as he found his own release.

For a long time the only sound in the room was their erratic, rasping breath; neither was capable of speech, until eventually Justin rolled on to his back and curved an arm around her shoulders, tucking her into his side.

'Justin, my love.' She sighed, turning her head to press a soft kiss to his sweat-dampened chest.

'Enough, Zoë. Lie still,' he ordered raggedly.

They were the first words he had spoken in ages, she realised, but, lying satiated beside him, she didn't mind. She loved her silent lover... Anyway, she made enough noise for both of them, she thought, slightly shocked at how Justin always managed to get her to beg for his possession. But then why shouldn't he? He was an experienced, sophisticated lover, and he was only making sure that she was satisfied, she rationalised contentedly. But her contentment plunged five minutes later...

'I'll leave you to sleep now, darling,' Justin murmured. Removing his arm from her shoulder, he swung his feet to the floor.

'Stay,' she drawled huskily.

But Justin stood up. Unselfconscious in his nudity, he turned to look down at where she lay in the rumpled bed. She gazed languidly up at him; her blue eyes, slumberous and dark with loving, met his. Then, as she watched, she saw his iron self-control reassert itself. His heavy lids dropped over his half-closed eyes as he moved slightly, avoiding her gaze.

'Much as I'd like to, it isn't sensible; I have to be up at six in the morning to be in London for eight. I would only disturb you, Zoë, and you need your rest.' He was talking to somewhere over her left shoulder—as usual! The thought was frightening ...

Zoë sat up in bed and reached out a detaining hand, placing it on his naked thigh. 'I could come to London with you.' His hand lifted hers from his thigh and she had the oddest notion that he resented her touch. 'We could move to your apartment n-now——' she swallowed the lump that formed in her throat "—now Uncle Bertie's gone.'

Suddenly it seemed imperative to her that they discuss the future, and she didn't know why. 'We can put this house on the market—it's far too big; it's an anachronism in this day and age. Never mind one child—we would need a dozen even to begin to fill it——'

'So that's what this is all about?' Justin cut in. "I thought we agreed—no babies for a year or two. You would not be trying to blackmail me into changing my mind by threatening to sell the house?' he demanded hardly. 'Because, if so, you can forget it.'

'No, no, nothing like that,' she quickly denied. But as she searched his face he looked so cool and remote that once more Sara Blacket's words echoed in her brain, filling her with a dawning fear that she did not want to recognise. Instead she continued, 'I simply thought that the house could be a conference centre or a nursing home—something like that. It is very expensive to keep up; Judge Master said so himself.' She knew she was babbling but she wanted to keep Justin with her.

He leant forward, brought her small hand to his lips and brushed her knuckles with a kiss. 'You're probably right and if you want to sell it I'll arrange it, but it's not something one can do in five minutes.' And, pressing another kiss on the back of her hand, he added, 'And let me worry about the expense, little one. You try and get some sleep.'

She should have been reassured, but somehow she wasn't. Maybe it was the way he avoided her eyes, or perhaps the way he allowed her hand to fall from his, but she had the strangest notion that he was simply pacifying her as he would a troublesome child.

'I will if you stay with me,' she said slowly. She was testing him, and hated herself for it, but the events of the day had severely dented her confidence in her husband's love and she needed some sign from him, freely given, to allay her doubts and fears.

'I need my sleep even if you don't. I'm a lot older than you, remember.'

'Please, Justin, I need you tonight, simply to hold me. What with the funeral...' She didn't want to plead, but somehow it had become essential to her peace of mind and her trust in him that just this once he stayed all night. To her relief and delight he agreed.

'Let me dispose of the protection.' He grinned. 'I'll be back in a second.'

And he was. Zoë yawned widely and snuggled into the hard warmth of her cautious husband's arms. 'You're not old,' she whispered, a smile twitching her swollen lips. It was ridiculous—a more virile, powerful man than her husband would be hard to find, and yet somehow the fact that he should worry about his age made him seem touchingly vulnerable. It never bothered her.

Justin, true to his word, had the house valued by a prestigious estate agent with a view to selling the place. But to Zoë's amazement Justin informed her, before they actually put it on the market, that she was to have her twenty-first birthday party at Black Gables. It was all arranged; the guests had already been invited.

Apparently Justin had done it at Bertie's request. It had been his last wish that the party go ahead whether he was there to see it or not. Zoë was not absolutely convinced that it was the right thing to do only three weeks after her uncle's death, but, as usual, she gave in to her dynamic husband's wishes.

The next few weeks she passed in a kind of limbo, torn between grief for her uncle and her inability to get really close to her husband.

Justin was very busy as the new head of chambers, and she saw less and less of him. She tried to tell herself it was natural—he had more work to get through. But sometimes in the evening, after yet another solitary dinner, a devilish, tiny voice from the deeper reaches of her mind would rise up to taunt her with the thought that he had married her to please Bertie and get the firm. He had the firm and Bertie was no longer around to see if he neglected his wife. She found it more and more difficult to dismiss her suspicions, however much she tried.

Justin was no help. He rarely talked about his work but he did inform her that he would be staying in town on Monday evenings. He had taken over the job of boxing coach with a group of young offenders at an East End boys' club. Very laudable—and she believed him even as she missed him. But her inability to dismiss completely the conversation she had overheard on the day of her uncle's funeral was a constant source of unease.

She was a practical girl—with egotistical film-star parents she had had to be from a very young age. She knew she was being silly, letting Sara Blacket's catty remarks get to her. Justin loved her. They were married for heaven's sake!

But, however much she tried to convince herself, the doubt lingered. It didn't help that Justin seemed to spend longer and longer in London. He was working far too hard, but nothing she said could make him change.

She was smiling as she spun the wheel of her Mini Metro and headed up the drive to come to a halt, with a screech of brakes, outside the front door of the house. She had spent the day in London, and had had the rare pleasure of lunching with her husband at an exclusive restaurant before raiding Harvey Nichols. The bag lying on the passenger seat contained the most exotic gown she had ever owned.

She picked up the carrier-bag and chuckled as she dashed out of the car and into the house. She could not wait to see Justin's face when he saw her new dress. She wouldn't give a cent for his iron control tomorrow night—her birthday party. The gown was guaranteed to knock him dead. But why did she need to? The question hovered on the fringes of her mind, undermining her confidence.

Not bad—not bad at all, she thought, posing naked in front of the mirrored wall of the bathroom, sucking in her stomach, her small breasts rising enticingly. Were they bigger than usual? she wondered idly. Probably Justin's expert massage was to blame. She giggled and, with a happy smile illuminating her small face, spun round as the object of her thoughts strolled in.

'I didn't hear you,' she said delightedly. She had not seen him since last night and her eyes drank in the sight of the large, splendid bulk of him, clad in a plain black towelling robe that stopped mid-thigh, the deep V of the front exposing his broad, hairy chest. Her heart jumped in her breast as, eyes shining, she walked towards him, 'You must have got back when I was in the shower.'

'Mmm,' Justin grunted, his gaze sweeping slowly over her silver-blonde hair, the perfect oval face, the finely arched brows, the huge, thick-lashed eyes, the small, straight nose and the wide full-lipped, rosy mouth, curved in a warm smile of welcome. His gaze lingered on the lips, then moved almost as if against his will down to the high, full breasts, the tiny waist and flat stomach, the softly flaring hips, his eyes darkening to black in the process.

Zoë, seeing his reaction and thrilled by it, moved closer and slipped a hand under the lapel of his robe. 'Thank you for the card and the roses. I love them,' she husked, thinking of the magnificent bouquet of red roses that had been delivered to the house earlier.

'My pleasure, birthday girl,' he drawled none too steadily.

She felt him tense as her fingernail scraped supposedly accidentally over a small, pebble-like male nipple. Perhaps she had been wrong about Justin; perhaps her fantasy of them in the shower was not so unlikely, she thought, excitement sizzling in her veins.

'Shall I help you to shower?' she asked throatily, glancing up at his tough face through the thick veil of her lashes in what she hoped was a seductive fashion.

His eyes flashed gold lightning as his arm swept around her waist and hauled her into his hard body, while his other hand caught her wandering one beneath his robe. 'You little devil,' he rasped, before covering her mouth with his own in a long, hard kiss.

When he finally released her she was dazed and breathless and aching. 'Justin...' She sighed his name. But, to her chagrin, he spun her round, patted her naked bottom, and almost pushed her out of the door.

'Tempting though the offer is, it's late. The guests will be arriving any minute. Get dressed and allow me to do the same.'

'Spoilsport,' she shouted back cheekily, regaining her equilibrium and shooting him a flirtatious glance over her shoulder.

Justin tossed back his black head and laughed out loud. 'Hold the thought till later, darling, when I have time to do it justice, hmm?'

His parting words filled her with confidence as she stood in front of the cheval-glass, turning this way and that, a complacent grin lighting her face. So much for a Dresden doll, she thought triumphantly. Tonight no one would be in any doubt she was all woman.

The black dress was like nothing she had ever owned before—a sophisticated designer original with tiny, narrow straps supporting the pure silk bodice. She wore no bra because the back was non-existent except for a very broad, sequin-encrusted belt in gold, which nipped her tiny waist and pushed her firm breasts higher— almost empire-style—revealing the curve of the milky white orbs and a tantalising shadowy cleavage.

The skirt was straight to her ankles and figure-hugging, with a teasing fish tail at the back. Matching four-inch-heel satin sandals on her feet gave her an illusion of height, as did the heavy sweep of her blonde hair piled up on the top of her head in a chignon, a few strands of hair pulled free to curl enticingly around her face and the back of her neck.

She did not need foundation, simply a good moisturiser and the lightest trace of blusher to add colour to her fine pale skin. She had paid more attention to her eyes, and, with the careful use of a coloured eyeshadow and the addition of a brownish-black mascara to her long lashes, she knew she had never looked better.

'My God! What on earth are you wearing?'

Justin's horrified cry broke into her reverie. She turned slowly around and spread her arms wide. 'Don't you like it?' she asked as she pirouetted again, then stopped in front of him, grinning wickedly up into his stunned face.

He looked magnificent in a black dinner-suit, white silk shirt and black bow-tie—all elegant, sophisticated male—and for once Zoë thought she matched him. But, if the look in his dark eyes was anything to go by, maybe she was wrong. She saw the muscle in his strong throat move as he swallowed hard. 'Justin?' she queried.

'Like it...? It's indecent. You will give every man in the place a heart attack—me included.' His dark gaze lingered on her shadowy cleavage. 'Why not wear the romantic thing you wore on Valentine night?' he suggested hoarsely.

'Don't be so staid,' she teased, adding, 'In any case, it's too late to change now.' She slipped her arm through his. 'Let's go down; we can't keep our guests waiting.'

'Wait.' He closed his large hand over hers and turned her towards him. 'I have something for you.' His eyes dipped to her breast and then returned to her face. One dark brow arched sardonically. 'Though I didn't have a neckline like that in mind when I bought it,' he said drily, slipping his free hand into his jacket pocket and withdrawing a long jewel case. He held it out to her.

She opened the box and gasped. 'It's unbelievable,' she cried, her eyes dazzled by the blaze from a magnificent diamond choker set with sapphires falling like tear-drops all around—a perfect match for her engagement ring.

'Happy birthday, Zoë.'

She looked up into her husband's dark, serious eyes, her own filling with moisture. How could she have ever doubted that he loved her? she thought wryly.

'I love it, Justin, as I love you. You darling man.' And, reaching up, she kissed the highest point she could reach—his chin. He pulled back almost as though he was embarrassed by her show of emotion. 'Please put it on for me,' she said in a voice that was not quite steady as she lifted the necklace from its bed of velvet and held it out to him.

He took it, his smouldering gaze intent upon her small face, then, moving behind her, fastened the necklace around her slender neck. Turning her back to face him, he said with arrogant certainty, 'I *knew* they would match your eyes.'

She put a hand to her throat. 'Thank you,' she murmured, her heart bursting with love.

'There is more,' he said softly, a tender grin quirking the corners of his sensuous mouth as he delved once more into his jacket pocket and withdrew a smaller case. 'From Bertie.'

She swallowed the lump that rose in her throat. 'How?' she whispered, taking the proffered box.

'He sent for the jeweller two months ago and chose it himself. I promised I would give it to you at the appropriate time.'

She opened the box and lifted out a delicate gold watch of startling beauty. The time markings on the face were etched in diamonds and the surround was encrusted in diamonds and sapphires. 'I wish he could have been here,' she whispered, fastening the watch around her slender wrist and raising tear-drenched eyes to her husband.

'He is in spirit, love.' Justin pulled her into his arms and gave her a quick hug. 'Dry your eyes and let's go.'

Ten minutes later Zoë, once again in control of her emotions, followed her husband into the formal drawing-room. 'I feel guilty allowing you to arrange all this for me—the party, the caterers.' She glanced at the watch on her wrist; any moment now the guests would be arriving. 'The guests.' And she stopped, her mouth falling open. She had forgotten to tell Justin...

'Justin, I—er—I hope you don't mind but——' She glanced at him leaning negligently against the French marble fireplace, the epitome of the sophisticated male animal, and hesitated.

'But what?' He arched one dark brow enquiringly.

'You know when I worked at Magnum Advertising? Well, I have kept in touch with some of the staff—an occasional lunch in town—and——' she took a deep breath '—a few of them are hiring a minibus and coming to the party,' she finished in a rush.

'Why not? Your uncle insisted on inviting everyone from the doorman at chambers to the Lord Chief Justice—a few more won't matter.' In two lithe strides he was beside her. 'Stop worrying. It is your party—enjoy it.'

She took a deep breath to steady her fluttering nerves. 'I'll try.'

'But for God's sake don't breathe like that in that apology for a gown!' he exclaimed irritably, and would have said more, if the thunderous expression on his dark face was anything to go by. But at that moment the doorbell chimed...

CHAPTER THREE

As ZOË stood in the huge old panelled hall with Justin at her side, his proprietorial arm around her waist, her doubts of the past few weeks vanished. She had never been happier as they greeted the constant flow of guests.

She welcomed Judge Master and his wife Mary with a kiss on their cheeks, while Justin looked indulgently on. She was not quite as enthusiastic with Sara Blacket and her husband, but soon she was having difficulty keeping track of who every one was.

Then, to her surprise, a tall, rangy stranger appeared, looking for all the world like a cowboy. She hesitated for a second, then let out a startled cry of joy. It had been seven years but there was no mistaking Wayne Sutton, the Texan. He had been a friend of her parents for years and she remembered him as being particularly kind to her when she was a child in California.

'Wayne, I can't believe it...' She grinned up into his deeply tanned, handsome face. 'How did you get here?'

'I walked on water of course,' he teased with masculine arrogance.

It would not have surprised her if he had. From being a rising young executive when her parents were alive he was now the head of one of the major studios in Hollywood, yet he couldn't have been much over forty.

'Let me look at *you*,' Wayne drawled provocatively and, casually pulling her out of her husband's arms, he held her hands wide and gave her a long, lingering scrutiny. 'You're more beautiful than your mother ever was. How about becoming a film star——?'

'Hands off!' Justin cut in, hauling her back to his side. 'The lady is spoken for, Wayne.' The two men held each other's gaze, sizing each other up rather like two stags at bay.

Zoë's puzzled eyes shot from one to the other. 'You know each other?'

'Wayne and I spoke on the telephone last week,' Justin said curtly. 'And he is here tonight in his capacity as the executor of your trust fund. Nothing more.'

'No business tonight, Wayne.' She deliberately spoke to the Texan, not at all happy with Justin's tone of voice. She reached up and kissed Wayne's cheek. 'I should scold you,' she teased. 'To think that you've spoken to my husband and yet not once have you got in touch with me!' She pouted, flirting outrageously.

'Hey, honey, that's not true. Surely you got my Valentine's cards? Damn it! I paid the agency in London enough for the service. I knew you would miss not getting one from your dad, so I kind of took his place.'

Her smile faltered. All these years it had been Wayne and not Justin... 'Yes, yes, of course. Thank you, Wayne; I appreciated the gesture; I just forgot.' She felt the colour rise in her face and quickly changed the subject. 'But come on; you're here to enjoy yourself— bar's second door on the left and there's champagne everywhere.' She indicated the hovering waiters balancing trays loaded with glasses of champagne.

'Whatever you say, gorgeous.' Wayne winked. 'Now, let me find the bourbon.' And he walked off towards the bar.

Justin's skin darkened with colour. 'There was no need to kiss the man.'

'Why, I do believe you're jealous!' Zoë teased. She was stupidly hurt to discover after all these years that the cards had not come from Justin, but she was determined not to show it.

'It's that damned dress,' Justin bent down to murmur in her ear. 'Every time you reach up, I have palpitations in case you pop out the top.'

She glanced up, her eyes clashing with his. His show of possession was flattering, and she laughed out loud, her humour restored. To the people watching, the stern barrister's responding laughter came as something of a shock.

For the rest of the introductions Zoë relaxed easily in her husband's hold, until she felt Justin tense, his fingers tightening imperceptibly on her waist. She shot him a sidelong glance; his rugged features were set in an impassive mask. She looked back to the couple in front of her. She knew the man, Bob Oliver, a junior partner in the law firm; her glance shifted to his red-headed companion, and immediately she knew the reason for Justin's sudden tension. Janet Ord had been his companion at Zoë's eighteenth birthday...

'Bob and Janet, how nice to see you again; it must be three years.' She tried to lighten the atmosphere. She was Justin's wife and she wanted to show him that she was adult enough to realise that it was only to be expected that eventually she would bump into one of his old girlfriends. The law, and those who pursued it in England, comprised quite an insular community.

'Good to see you, Bob—Janet.'

She heard Justin's voice, cool and clipped, and wondered at the unmistakable frostiness in his tone. But at that moment the busload of friends from Magnum Advertising arrived, and she forgot all about Justin's peculiar reticence with his junior partner and Janet. A few hours later she was to remember and wonder how she could have been such a fool...

She looked around the crowded room, her blue eyes shining like stars. The party was going brilliantly; the caterers had done a superb job on the buffet and the large formal dining-room was subjected to a constant stream of guests. In the small ballroom, opened for the first time in years for the occasion, an enthusiastic quintet played a good mixture of popular and rock music.

'Quite a triumph,' Justin murmured, turning her into his arms and grinning down at her. 'Though I should be angry with you. You never mentioned the pipsqueak Nigel was one of your guests.'

'I could say the same,' she teased back, confident in his love. 'You never mentioned that the luscious Janet was invited.'

His grin vanished, his face going peculiarly rigid. 'I did not invite the lady. I ruined your eighteenth party by inviting that woman—do you really think I would be so unthinking as to repeat the mistake?'

Inexplicably she shivered.

'Zoë, you're cold. It's that damned dress.'

'No, no. A ghost walking over my grave.' She tried to smile. Or was it an omen? she wondered.

'Bob invited Janet as his partner. Do you mind?' Justin bit out, his dark gaze intent on her upturned face.

'No, of course not, silly.' She shrugged off her fanciful thoughts. 'Come on, let's dance.' And, curving her slender arms around his waist, she swayed in towards him.

Justin needed no second bidding, and she hid a secret smile as she noted his muffled sigh of relief when he urged her on to the dance-floor. Poor man! He was obviously afraid that she would take offence and sulk as she had three years ago.

They danced, Justin stroking one hand up her bare back while the other rested lightly on her hip. She flattened her palms on his shirt-front and gave herself up to the dreamy music, swaying to the rhythm of the golden oldie 'As Time Goes By'.

His hand moved from her hip to her buttock as he pulled her closer, one long leg edging between hers. She felt him stir against her, his hold tighten, and the familiar heat flowed through her. His dark head bent; his lips brushed lightly over her brow. She tilted her head back; their eyes met and desire lanced between them, as sharp and piercing as a laser-beam.

'How long will this damn party last?' he muttered as his hand moved up her back, his fingers spreading to clasp her nape while his other hand dropped to stroke her thigh.

She made no response; instead she simply gazed dazedly up at him, her pulse racing. Her husband's control was slipping, she thought bemusedly. They were lost in a world of their own; the crowd, the laughter faded away, and there was only passion and need. Then Justin kissed her...

It was the cheers of the guests and the heavy beat of a rock and roll number that brought them back to their senses.

Justin's head jerked back, his dark face flushed with passion and a good deal of embarrassment as he shot a frustrated glance at the assembled throng. 'I need a drink. *We* need a drink,' he muttered, his arms falling to his sides. 'I knew that dress was a disaster area. I should never have allowed you to wear it,' he growled angrily.

She regained her composure—for once, before her dynamic husband—and her lips twitched in the beginnings of a smile. 'Why, I do believe, Mr Gifford——' she held his gaze, fluttering her long eyelashes like some Southern belle '—your behaviour is most unbecoming for a barrister and soon-to-be judge,' she drawled in mock-horror, and then spoilt it by giggling.

'Witch!' Justin chuckled. 'I'll get you later; meanwhile I think we should circulate. It will be much easier on my libido.'

She glanced around the dance-floor, rubbing one foot against her ankle: four-inch heels gave her height, but they played havoc with her feet. She had danced with dozens of men, including the Lord Chief Justice. She had done her duty, and with a cheerful smile to everyone in general she escaped out into the hall, and went on through the garden-room, where a few close couples were in conversation, and into the old-fashioned Victorian conservatory.

Good! She was alone. She sank down on to a bamboo chair—part of a group placed around a centre table. She slipped off her shoes, put her feet inelegantly on the glass table in front of her and let her head fall back against the soft cushion. Five minutes' rest and then back to the fray, she promised herself.

It was a beautiful summer night and through the glass roof a million stars glittered in the midnight-blue sky. She sighed deeply, contentedly. Twenty-one on the twenty-first of June—there must be a lucky omen in there somewhere, she mused, not that she needed luck; she had it all ...

'Hiding, Zoë.' A feminine voice interrupted her reverie. She glanced up and muffled a groan as Janet swayed unsteadily before her.

'No. Simply resting for a minute or two.'

'I don't blame you.' The redhead collapsed in the opposite chair, a glass in one hand and a half-full bottle of champagne in the other.

Zoë thought, So much for my five minutes' peace. 'I hope you're enjoying the party,' she prompted with a tinge of sarcasm. The woman was obviously three sheets to the wind.

'Great party.' Janet giggled and took a swig of the champagne, ignoring the glass and drinking from the bottle. 'But, parties aside, I can understand your needing a rest. Just—J-ustin is one dynamic lover—a tiger in bed.' She took another swig of the champagne.

Zoë didn't want to hear any more. It was one thing to accept that your husband had had lovers in the past, but quite another to have one of the same describe his powers in bed. 'Yes, well . . .' she mumbled, praying that the other woman would leave or pass out. But her wish wasn't granted.

'Def-f-f . . . Definit-t-t . . .' Janet slurred the words. 'A three-times-a-night man, and day, and anywhere.' Her high-pitched laughter grated across Zoë's nerves like a dentist's high-powered drill.

'"A three-times-a-night man" . . .' Zoë whispered, shocked to the core. She knew what it meant, and could not believe they were talking about the same person. They made love most nights but Justin was always in control, and they never did it more than once. Well, except for the night of the funeral, she qualified in her mind.

Suddenly her confidence in her husband's love took a nosedive. She remembered the conversation she had overheard—Sara Blacket's opinion that Justin preferred large, luscious women.

She looked across at Janet. Had she been the redhead at the dinner Mrs Blacket had mentioned? It was possible. Janet was a very attractive, very well-endowed sexy woman of about Justin's age; add to that the fact that they had once worked in the same chambers and three years ago they had arrived as a couple at her eighteenth birthday and it made sense. Justin and this woman had been lovers not for a few weeks, as Zoë had mistakenly imagined, but for years . . .

'He's not the sort to go without, not our Justin.'

Zoë raised huge blue eyes to the other woman's face; she was still talking, but Zoë felt as if she had been hit by a truck. 'No?' she queried numbly.

'Even the night before he got married I had to throw him out of my place at two in the morning—couldn't have him exhausted for his wedding... No, sir... So keep your strength up, girl; you'll need it.' And, leaning across the table, she held out the bottle of champagne. 'Have a drink...'

Zoë blindly shook her head. She could not believe Janet. She didn't want to, but as Janet rambled on she was filled with a certain dread.

'Don't get me wrong, I like Justin.' Janet fell back against the seat. 'He's ambitious; he could have stayed with our firm—become a top international lawyer, loads of money. But he preferred the establishment. He wants the prestige of the ermine. Already head of your late uncle's firm, he will be a faithful husband. He has no choice if he wants to make judge. You have nothing to worry about. Nothing at all...'

Deep inside Zoë something shattered—something rare and pure, an intrinsic part of her—her faith and love in her husband. She sat as though carved in stone, robbed of her pride and self-respect by the casual words of a drunken woman. She bit her lip to prevent the scream of anguish that was filling her head; she could almost hear the dull beat of her too trusting heart echoing in a black void.

'There you are, Janet. I've been looking all over for you.' Bob's voice intruded in the silence. His handsome, boyish face wreathed in smiles, he took the bottle from Janet's hand and placed it on the table, and, grabbing her arm, pulled her to her feet. 'You've had enough.'

Only then did he see Zoë.

'The party girl, having a breather.' He put a finger to his lips. 'Shh. We'll leave you to it.'

Bob's smiling face swam before her eyes, and she tried to smile. 'It's OK Bob; I just have to put my shoes on and I'll be back inside.'

The effort it took her to get the words out was more than she could stand. She slid her feet off the table and bent over, her head almost in her lap, more to hide the tears in her eyes than from any real desire to find her shoes.

She heard the other two depart, and her arms fell towards the floor, her hands shaking; she felt around in the semi-darkness for her sandals.

Slipping her feet back into the sandals, she stood up. The faint noise of the party filtered through her stunned brain. Her party. Her twenty-first, on the twenty-first... So much for lucky omens! If twenty-one was coming of age, she had come of age with a vengeance in the last ten minutes, she thought bitterly, dashing the tears from her cheeks with an angry, shaking hand.

Janet's revelation and all Zoë's niggling doubts and fears of the past few weeks coalesced into one absolute certainty: whatever reason Justin had for marrying her, it had not been love...

She straightened her shoulders and took a deep breath; she could hear her name being called. Now was not the time to give way to the pain gnawing at her heart. Instead she smoothed the soft silk of her dress down over her hips, adjusted the bodice and, with head held high, a smile plastered on her face, walked back into the garden-room.

'There you are, Zoë. I was looking all over for you.'

It was Wayne, thank God! Right at that minute she didn't think she could have faced Justin.

'Sorry to be a party-pooper, but I have to get back to London; I have a breakfast meeting in the morning. But I would like to arrange a meeting with you, Zoë. We have a lot to discuss—the trust, the transfer of the cash.

And I want to fly back Thursday; I must be at the studio on Friday.'

'Wayne, please.' The idea came to her in a flash. She glanced up into his tanned, attractive face. She could trust this man—that much she was sure of. She placed her hand on his arm, her wide blue eyes, unbeknown to her, betraying her pain and anguish. 'It was lovely to see you, but there's no need for us to meet in London. Don't transfer anything. I'll be in the States in a few days and I'll call you at the studio.'

'Zoë, what's wrong?' The Texan's tanned hand touched her shoulder in a gesture of comfort. 'You're shivering—something has upset you. I know I haven't seen you in years, but you can trust me; your parents were my friends. If anyone has hurt you, tell me, and I'll punch their lights out.'

His kindness and insight were almost her undoing. 'Please, Wayne, don't ask questions, and promise you won't mention any of this to...to—' she couldn't say his name '—to my husband.'

'You've got it, honey. I'll wait for your call.' And, bending down, he planted a swift kiss on her cheek. 'Chin up, kid. Remember your parents were great actors; you can do it.'

'Wayne, you're wonderful. Come on, I'll see you out.' And with her arm linked in his she made it to the hall and the front door. They said goodbye with another brief kiss, and she was just about to turn around when Justin's voice reached her.

'Zoë, darling, I was beginning to think I had lost you.'

You have, you bastard! Pain and rage almost blinded her, but she bit her tongue and said nothing, suffering Justin's hand on her arm as he turned her around.

'The Lord Chief Justice and his wife are about to leave; they want to say goodnight.'

'But of course. You can't afford to upset Justice Speak,' she said with biting sarcasm.

'Zoë...' Justin began.

'Lovely party.' Justice Speak strolled up, his wife clinging to his arm. 'Sorry to leave, but at our age we need our rest.' He chuckled.

'Thank you for coming, and for the wonderful present—I shall cherish it always,' Zoë responded politely, and she wasn't lying. She did love the exquisite gold miniature they had given her.

'Glad you like it, my dear. Your uncle Bertie advised me—rang me the week before he died and told me you loved art. Great friend, sorry to lose him.' The old man's voice was gruff. 'He was so proud of you, young woman, and so pleased he had got you and Justin together; he could die content.'

Moisture filled her eyes—for her uncle, but also for herself. Dear heaven! Even Justice Speak knew her marriage had been arranged. Did everyone? Was she the only idiot who had not seen the truth?

'There, there, girl, don't upset yourself. Bertie would have loved to have seen the old house lit up and full of laughter again. I don't suppose you knew his wife, but she was a wonderful woman—loved entertaining on the grand scale; after she died Bertie rather let the place go.' The old man chattered on. 'Can't say I blame him—different era, don't you know! But you gave him a new lease on life; he adored you.'

Justin's arm curved around her waist and she stiffened immediately. Wiping the tears from her eyes, she forced a smile to her lips. 'Yes, I know; this party was his idea. So thank you once again for coming,' she managed to say firmly.

The goodnights said, a steady stream of guests began leaving until by two in the morning only her friends from Magnum Advertising were left. Zoë was reluctant for them to go and insisted on sharing another couple of bottles of champagne. The idea of getting drunk held great appeal. It might anaesthetise her feelings, so that she would not feel the pain she knew was waiting for her the moment she relaxed.

She was sitting on the sofa listening to one of Nigel's shaggy-dog stories—something he was renowned for—and sipping her drink, when Justin walked into the room, having dismissed the band.

He took in the scene at a glance—Zoë and Nigel on the sofa, two of the girls sprawled on the floor at their feet. Pat and Pam, Zoë's luncheon friends, were almost asleep on the other sofa. His dark gaze sought hers but she avoided his eyes. She couldn't bear to look at him. She sensed him move towards her, and only looked up when he spoke.

'Sorry, folks, the driver is insisting on leaving. Time to go.'

'We have the room. They can stay the night.'

'I don't think so, Zoë. They have to work tomorrow.'

'The master has spoken,' Nigel quipped, getting to his feet and performing a rather drunken salute. But the rest followed suit.

Zoë smiled grimly, her gaze colliding with her husband's and moving as quickly away again. Nigel was closer to the truth than he knew. 'Yes, indeed,' she concurred, standing up, and, ignoring Justin's narrow-eyed scrutiny, she followed the last of the guests to the hall and bid them goodnight.

'What was all that about?' Justin demanded hardly, catching her arm when she would have walked straight past him to the stairs.

She glanced down at his long fingers curled around her arm, and then tilted back her head to stare a long way up into his harsh face. 'I don't know what you mean,' she said flatly, proud of her self-control when really she felt like tearing his eyes out. 'I'm tired; I'm going to bed. Lock up, won't you?'

'Zoë, don't lie to me. Something is wrong.' He moved closer and she flinched.

'You're being ridiculous,' she snapped; she could not stand his questioning much longer.

'I think not.' He was inches away, his tall figure dwarfing her. She could almost see his analytical mind going over the events of the evening. 'The party was great, you were enjoying yourself, and then I lost sight of you for a while. When I saw you again you were kissing Wayne, and then you could barely speak to me, and for the rest of the night you flirted with Nigel while treating me as if I were some kind of ogre. What happened, Zoë? Did someone say something to upset you?'

She could have wept. 'Upset' wasn't the word. 'Destroyed' maybe! She glared at him, hurt and fury warring within her. He looked so cool, so in control, even concerned! Uncle Bertie had once told her that the truly great barristers could just as easily be actors, the court the stage, and the judge and jury the audience, and, by God, Justin should have received an academy award for the part he had played for years!

'Answer me, Zoë.' His fingers tightened on her arm.

'No one upset me; I had a wonderful evening and you have an over-active imagination,' she declared flatly. She had to get away; his closeness, the subtle scent of him were draining her will-power. 'You're also hurting my arm.'

His hand fell away immediately. 'Sorry,' he apologised and, stuffing his hands in his pockets, his voice terse, he added, 'Perhaps you're right. Go to bed; I'll be up in a minute.'

Glad to escape, she kicked off her shoes and ran up the stairs. She closed the bedroom door behind her and quite deliberately locked it. She tore off her clothes and left them where they fell; her jewellery she dropped in a heap on the dressing-table along with the key and then she dashed into the bathroom and locked the door to Justin's room before stepping into the shower.

She lifted her head and allowed the fierce pressure of the water to wash over her, in the vain hope that it would wash away her tormented thoughts. Her tears mingled with the spray and, hating her own vulnerability, she turned off the water and stepped out of the shower. She wrapped a large soft towel around her naked body, sarong-style, and sank down on the small bathroom stool, burying her head in her hands. Her long, wet hair, hanging in tangled rats' tails down over her shoulders, dripped, unnoticed, on her rapidly cooling flesh.

Sara Blacket had been right all along. Justin had married her to please her uncle and further his career. His real preference was for large, luscious ladies and Janet Ord had confirmed the fact in a few short sentences.

Zoë groaned out loud. Justin! 'A three-times-a-night man'. How could she have been so naïve? The pain in her heart was worse than any knife wound—it went through flesh and blood to her very soul. Justin—her husband, her lover, who had only spent the whole night with her once since their wedding night—the night of the funeral—and even then she had had to beg him to stay and comfort her. She felt so stupid. So *used* ...

With hindsight it was all so obvious. Justin made love to her with a skill and sophistication she was helpless to resist—had never wanted to resist. But now she realised how naïve she had been. She had thought the fact that Justin always brought her to a shattering climax before finding his own release was the ultimate act of love by a considerate husband. Now she saw it for what it was—a clinical manipulation of her body and her love for him, while never losing his own iron control.

Being brutally honest with herself, she knew deep down inside that she had recognised that Justin held some part of himself back, but had refused to face the knowledge until now. She had masked it by telling herself that it was solely a cultural difference. She had spent her formative years used to the easy friendship and the exuberant, extrovert types of people who had made up her parents' circle of friends. Justin's attitude was simply very British and nothing to worry about—the stiff upper lip, and all that, not the most tactile of people.

She raised her head and shivered; the water running from her hair was freezing her tender flesh, but she welcomed the numbness. She heard a sound and glanced at the door to Justin's room—the handle was moving. She thanked God that she had locked the door; she could not face him—not tonight. She hadn't the strength. She had a terrible suspicion that if he took her in his arms and kissed her she would be the same spineless pushover she had always been where he was concerned.

Sadly she realised her own weakness. Every night in Justin's arms was her idea of heaven. She could have forgiven him the steely control, the separate beds, even his ambition and conniving with Uncle Bertie to marry her. But what she could not forgive—could not live with!—was Janet Ord's last revelation.

No man who had any respect at all for his prospective bride—never mind love—would ever spend the eve of his wedding making love to another woman. To Zoë it was far worse than an unfaithful husband. If a married man went astray one presumed that he had at least tried to honour his commitment. Justin had not even tried; he had betrayed her on the eve—no, not the eve but the *morning* of her wedding, if Janet was to be believed . . . and Zoë did believe her.

''*In vino veritas*,'' Zoë sighed, getting to her feet, her mind made up. Nigel had been right when he'd called

Justin 'the Master'. Justin, except for one brief mistake three years ago, had masterminded her whole life for virtually the last seven years.

But no more... Her rose-coloured spectacles were smashed to smithereens, and she could see Justin for what he was—a ruthlessly ambitious, mature male who had taken one look at a shy fourteen-year-old girl and deliberately used her schoolgirl crush to bind her to him in matrimony and further his career in the process. She could not blame him for her uncle's heart attack, but he had certainly used it to his own advantage.

It had forced her back into his sphere of influence and it had been Justin who'd suggested that she give up her fledgling career in advertising immediately after he had made love to her on Valentine's night. She could not believe how stupid she had been. How corny can you get? she thought cynically. Justin had seduced her with red roses and soft words, the Ritz, romance and champagne, and she had swallowed the whole fantasy, believing in the omens of love...

Well, they said life went in seven-year cycles, she thought fatalistically. It was certainly true for her. At seven, boarding-school in Maine; at fourteen, England and Justin. Now, at twenty-one...back to America...

Who knew? she mused. Perhaps her subconscious mind had accepted the end of her marriage and had been working out the solution within minutes of Janet Ord opening her mouth, maybe even earlier—when Sara Blacket had planted the first seeds of doubt in her heart.

With stark clarity she saw her impulsive declaration to Wayne—that she would see him in the States in a matter of days—as the best and only solution.

Tightening the towel around her breasts, and flicking her wet hair from her eyes, she moved like an old woman to the door and into her room.

CHAPTER FOUR

ZOË clutched at the door-frame with one hand and her towel with the other. Her heart almost stopped beating, and her eyes widened in angry shock at the sight before her.

In the dim glow of the bedside light Justin was sprawled across her bed. The pillows bunched behind his back to keep him semi-upright, he had a glass of champagne in his hand, a wicked light in his deep brown eyes, his only concession to modesty a pair of black silk boxer shorts. 'Short' being the operative word...

'I thought the black dress was a turn-on,' he drawled throatily, 'but that towel takes some beating.' Playfully crooking a finger, a sensual smile curving his wide mouth, he added, 'Come to bed, birthday girl. Let's celebrate.'

A few hours ago she would have been overjoyed at such a blatant statement of intent from her restrained husband, but with Janet's revelation in the forefront of her mind all she felt was a furious rage.

Obviously she had not hidden her distress as well as she had thought. Justin had picked up on it, she told herself with a new cynical awareness that she had not realised she possessed. Or why else would he, for the first time ever, be lying in wait for her? Except to get her in his arms and mindless as usual.

Her gaze slid slowly over him. He lay there, a sophisticated male animal, all rippling muscle and confident virile charm, expecting her to fall gratefully into his arms.

Well, the manipulative swine was in for a rude awakening.

'Celebrate? I think not,' she bit out, her lashes flickering over wild blue eyes to hide her fury. She deliberately turned, proceeded across the room to the dressing-table, and sat down on the softly padded stool, her glance resting on the key she had thrown down earlier.

'How did you get in?' She had locked the door, she knew she had...

'I know you didn't intend to lock me out, darling, and I also know all the locks in the master suite are the same. Open with the same key. *Et voilá*! Here I am.'

'I'm not in the mood for you or French, so please leave.'

'Zoë, what's wrong?' Justin swung his feet to the floor and in a couple of lithe strides was standing behind her.

'I'm tired. I want to sleep,' she said curtly, his towering presence at her back causing her stomach to knot with tension. If he touched her she'd scream...

'Funny—half an hour ago, you were almost begging Nigel and his friends to stay longer,' he reminded her silkily. 'A more suspicious husband might have cause for alarm.'

His hands curved over her naked shoulders, and she stiffened. She looked up, her gaze colliding in the mirror with dark, piercing eyes.

She had thought that every ounce of feeling for Justin had been destroyed by the knowledge she had gained this evening, but she was horrified to discover that, despite knowing that he had never loved her, that he had married her for ambition and at her uncle's request, his closeness and the touch of his hand could still arouse an aching longing inside her. She despised her own weakness, and in a fury of hurt and humiliation she jumped to her feet and swung away from him.

'A more suspicious wife might wonder why a new husband would prefer his own bed to his wife's,' she shot back scathingly.

An unfathomable expression flickered in his eyes; as she watched his mouth tightened. 'I didn't prefer my own bed tonight, but it doesn't seem to have done me much good,' he opined drily, an odd grating in his usually deep, modulated tone.

'About as much good as it does me, knowing you married me at my uncle Bertie's request, and simply to further your overriding ambition in law.' Not bothering to hide the bitterness in her voice, she spun to face him, head high. Her blue eyes shooting flames, she instantly dismissed his shocked expression as simply more play-acting.

'That is a ridiculous notion and patently untrue,' he denied harshly.

At one time Zoë might have believed him, but not any more. 'No?' One brow arched derisively. 'You mean Uncle Bertie never suggested to you that marrying me would please him?' If Zoë had any lingering doubts they vanished as Justin's glance seemed to waver, a dull flush streaking his high cheekbones.

'Zoë, I don't know what you have heard or who has been gossiping but it wasn't like that and you know it.'

'Oh, sure I know it! Next you'll be telling me you love me—something you have studiously avoided saying, and I was too stupid to see it.'

The one time she had asked him if he loved her—the day of the funeral—he had answered with, 'Of course I do, silly girl; I married you, didn't I?' At the time she had been reassured; now she saw it for the evasion it was.

'Zoë, what is going on here? It's not like you to deliberately try and start an argument.'

'You're right, it isn't, and I'm not about to argue with you now.' He was standing before her, all aggrieved, near-naked male, and she didn't trust herself not to reach out and stroke the muscular chest, to give in weakly to his overwhelming sex appeal. 'Just go,' she said sadly, tearing her eyes away from his powerful body.

'That's it!' The words exploded into the air like gunfire, and she stepped back in shocked surprise.

But Justin moved in on her. 'I don't know who has been filling your pretty little head with nonsense, but you and I are going to have a talk,' he grated between clenched teeth, and, taking her arm in a tight grip, marched her across to the bed.

'Let go of me!' she snapped angrily, trying to break free. But his fingers merely tightened on her tender flesh and she had to bite her lip to prevent a cry of pain.

'Sit down,' Justin ordered, pushing her down on the bed.

'Resorting to violence now, you hypocritical swine?' she accused seathingly.

'Be quiet,' he barked, and the leashed fury in his tone made her shiver inwardly as he stood towering menacingly over her. 'At the beginning of this evening everything between us was fine; in fact, it was only lack of time that prevented you and me sharing this bed earlier—you were aching for me.' An arrogant, knowing smile played across his mouth.

'I——' She tried to deny it, but he cut her off.

'Don't bother to lie,' he said curtly. 'I'm a man, Zoë; I know when a woman's responding to me. Just tell me what happened between then and now that you should accuse me of some ulterior motive for marrying you and deliberately give me the brush-off as if I had some anti-social disease, damn it!'

She looked up, her gaze slanting over his broad chest and on to his hard face and the dark, probing eyes which looked as if they could read her mind. His anger was genuine, but probably simply because she had found him out, she thought cynically.

'Do you deny you discussed marrying me with Uncle Bertie?' she asked, and, without giving him time to answer, carried on, 'Or that our marriage helped you become head of chambers?' She did not see his brown eyes leap with rage; she was too engrossed with her own, furious pain. 'Or that you kept your mistress—lover—call her what you like—right up to our wedding and probably beyond?'

'Stop right there!' Justin snarled. He leaned over her, his hands on either side of her on the bed, imprisoning her, forcing her to lean back with her hands behind her for support. He was so close that she could see the beginnings of dark stubble on his chin.

'Janet—that's what this is all about. She has been spreading her poison, and you, my trusting little wife, believed her,' he drawled in a dangerously quiet voice. 'Such loyalty! I think you owe me an apology and an explanation.'

He was actually serious! She could see that. The nerve of the beast. 'Try the "tiger in bed" for starters,' she spat back.

Her throat ached from the prolonged effort of holding back the tears, and her pulse raced as she fought to retain her composure. She was helplessly aware of her own embarrassing position—naked except for a towel—and Justin—much the same, with his keen eyes surveying her insolently from head to breast and lower. She felt the heat ignite in her stomach and silently cursed her body's unwelcome response to him.

'I don't believe it! You're jealous,' he marvelled. 'That's what all this is about.'

'In your dreams!' she cried furiously. 'I don't give a damn if you spend the rest of your life with the woman. I never want to see you again.'

The colour drained from his face. 'Zoë, you don't know what you're saying.' He looked at her seriously. 'You're my wife; I love you...' And that was the unkindest cut of all for Zoë—his declaration of love had come too late and sounded like the excuse it was.

'Since when?' she snorted. 'Since I found out the truth about you, you manipulative, chauvinistic pig?' She struggled to sit up, pushing at his chest. Surprisingly he moved and sat alongside her on the bed; she saw him clench and unclench his hands as if weighing up the prospect of putting them around her neck.

'Not the best response to a declaration of love,' he drawled, and smiled, not very pleasantly. '"Underwhelmed" would be an accurate description, though I think I can understand. Knowing Janet, she can be a very persuasive if poisonous lady.'

'You should know—you're the expert on the woman,' she cried. She could not stand much more. What was the point? she thought morosely, and made to stand up but Justin's arm fell around her shoulders, his hand gripping her upper arm tightly, as if by the pressure of his fingers he could convince her.

'I promise you, Zoë, Janet means nothing to me. I'm thirty-five; there have been other women in my life I admit, but not as many as you seem to think, and certainly nothing serious.' He sounded very calm and controlled and it only served to infuriate her further.

'Says you,' she spat.

The brown eyes narrowed angrily, but his voice remained cool and reasonable as he continued, 'I had an affair with Janet—if one could call it that. Two adults sharing an evening out and sex occasionally, that was all it was, and it was finished long before you and I married.'

She tilted her head to the side and stared at him, eyes wide and wild. 'You swine!' she hissed, her face alive with hatred.

'You're being childish, Zoë——'

'Long before we were married?' she cut in incredulously. 'You take me for a child, a complete idiot!' Her temper ran out of control and her voice shook. 'Maybe, if I was crazy enough about you, I could forget your cosy-cosy arrangement with my uncle; maybe live with the fact that you never loved me as I loved you. But as for the rest...' The words came out harsh with pent-up emotion. 'To have a woman tell me that my husband is a "three-times-a-night man" and more! This same husband who cannot bear to spend a night in the same bed as me. You make me sick...'

Zoë shook her head; she tried to go on, but her voice seemed to have dried up. Her heart pounded in her chest and she felt physically sick. But what did it matter? What more was there to say? Except that she was leaving him, and that much must be self-evident to Justin. But to her amazement he threw back his head and laughed out loud.

'You are jealous, sexually jealous, you silly girl. You have no need to be. Janet was obviously just trying to upset you and you fell for it.'

She couldn't believe the man; he was a lawyer, supposedly intelligent, and he actually thought it was a huge joke, even to the extent that there was smug satisfaction in his grinning countenance. A red haze blurred her vision and she struck out at his face with a wildly swinging hand. 'Well, fall for this, buster!' she yelled. 'I'm leaving you. You're the lawyer... Fix the divorce...'

Suddenly his hand tightened around her shoulders. 'This has gone far enough,' he muttered savagely. 'If you won't listen to reason, I'll have to convince you another way.' His other hand captured her chin and forced her head up and his mouth swooped on hers, prising her lips apart, savaging her soft mouth.

With her bent back over his arm, his hand sliding from her chin to tangle in her long hair, he held her fast as he ground his mouth over hers with ruthless passion. She lashed out at him with her fists and tried to drag her head away, a low moan escaping her at the pain he was inflicting.

Justin laughed, a harsh, guttural sound in the silence of the room. 'And I thought I was being considerate.' His tone was ironic, but the blazing fury in his eyes as he stared at her belied his cool voice.

'Considerate? Don't make me laugh,' she yelled hysterically, and struggled to escape, her arms flailing wildly, but he was far too quick and, catching her arms at the wrist, with a swivel of his hard body she was pinned back against the bed, her hands forced above her head in one of his.

She cried out, but his mouth swallowed the sound, his teeth biting into her lips while his other hand tore the towel from her body. She felt his long fingers close around her breast and shuddered.

His dark head lifted as he stared down at the pale skin laid bare to his hot eyes. His strong fingers moved slowly, squeezing the soft flesh; his thumb brushed the hardening tip, and his eyes flicked to her face.

'No, no.' She tremblingly shook her head and tried to fight him, her body bucking against him. She would not let him do this to her—never again, she vowed, even as her traitorous flesh cried out for his familiar touch.

'Yes, my love,' he drawled sardonically in a strangely thickened voice. 'You say you're leaving. You implied I never wanted you. Our lovemaking was less than perfect for you.' He straddled her thighs, his long, near-naked body poised over her. 'I intend to prove you wrong.'

And his head came down to take the place of his fingers at her breast.

'No. I don't want you.' She thought bitterly of Janet even as her heart thudded in her breast. 'Try Janet. I'm sure...' She ended on a groan, hurting with the intolerable pressure of trying to resist him when a slow-burning fire was licking through her body.

He flashed a glance at her wildly shaking head and she arched again, trying to throw him off, but only succeeded in prolonging the agony as her breasts brushed against the hard wall of his chest. He drew a harsh breath, forcing her head back to the bed with the pressure of his mouth, and when he finally freed her swollen lips she was shaking all over.

'Anyone can have Janet, but only I have you,' he snarled close to her ear. 'And that's the way it's going to stay.'

'No, no, no...' she breathed raggedly.

'Yes, yes, yes,' he mocked harshly as his body shifted to crush her deeply in the bed.

There was no doubt that Justin wanted her. Zoë, twisting and struggling beneath him, trying to dislodge the hardening weight of his body, recognised that fact even before he responded by thrusting one of his legs between hers. But she also knew that whatever his reasons, it wasn't love.

Her wide, angry eyes clashed with his, and what she saw in the black depths was a wild, savage, almost desperate hunger, and it shook her to the core. Gone was the controlled Justin she knew...

'I won't let you go. I can't,' he groaned, his mouth claiming hers once more as his hand trailed down across her breasts to the soft mound at her thighs.

Frantically she tried to struggle free, but the mental bonds were as strong if not stronger than the physical. She moaned as Justin buried his head at her throat, trailing moist kisses down to her breast while his hand parted her legs. She could feel the rigid, masculine length of him poised near the juncture of her thighs and she gasped as his long fingers slid between her silken, feminine folds. She was lost...

'Justin...'

His fingers moved intimately against her and she melted, liquid and hot, but he made no move to take possession. Instead he lifted his head from her breast, and stared down into her passion-flushed face.

'You can't win, Zoë, so stop fighting.' He groaned. His head lowering, he kissed her long and deeply.

'Fighting'? She clung to him, the nails of one hand biting into his shoulder, while those of the other scraped over his flat belly, tearing at his shorts. 'Who's fighting...?' She moaned as Justin shrugged out of his shorts and fell back on her, slipping between her parted thighs. She could no more control her body's reaction to him than fly to the moon.

'You want me...' he growled, and she could not deny it as he sheathed himself deeply inside her, covering her cry of excitement with his mouth.

Zoë glanced at the sleeping man beside her. His black hair was wet with sweat and plastered against his skull; his strong-featured face looked years younger in repose, the thick black lashes brushing his cheeks, masking the usually piercing, intelligent eyes.

She stirred restlessly in the bed, her body aching in places and muscles she doubted she had ever used before, or ever would again... The early morning sun shone through the windows, flooding the room with the palest of primrose light.

It was going to be a nice day. The inconsequential thought flashed in her mind. The English always moaned about the weather, and yet she had never found it too bad; in fact, she had adapted to the climate with no bother at all.

Maybe that was her trouble—she had been far too pliable, adapting to her uncle and Justin in much the same way as she had to the weather, a young girl desperate to be accepted by the only family she had left. A psychiatrist would probably have a field-day with the past seven years of her life.

She lifted her hand to her head and swept the tangled mass of her sweat-wet hair from her brow. She was naked, exhausted, sated, and yet unable to sleep. The last few hours had been a revelation to her. Justin had made love to her with a demanding, savage intensity that surpassed anything that had gone before.

To her amazement, and shame, she had matched him every time. Lost in a mindless frenzy, she had held him, shared with him, and followed him down a dozen erotic paths she had never dreamed of, until finally, with the light of dawn just breaking, he had fallen asleep. .

She glanced once more at him. A twisted smile curved her full lips but never reached her icy blue eyes. The irony did not escape her—only the threat of divorce could persuade her husband to spend all night in her bed. Nor could she avoid concluding that Janet had been right about her husband. He was a three-times-a-night man and more. But it also underlined the fact that Janet had been telling the truth...

A tear slowly trickled down her cheek; she sniffed and, turning, buried her head in the pillow. A strong arm fell over her waist and hauled her into the hard warmth of a masculine body. She swallowed hard; the last thing she wanted was that Justin should find her crying.

She lay tense and silent, expecting any second to hear him speak, but after a while she realised it had simply been a reflex action—he was still asleep. She stifled a yawn and closed her eyes; she was tired, so very tired.

At least in sleep she would not feel the pain of his betrayal, was her last conscious thought.

The following night the pain was still eating into Zoë's heart, tearing at her stomach, preventing her from eating. She shoved her chair back from the dinner-table and stood up.

'Do you want coffee in the study?' She addressed the question to somewhere over Justin's left shoulder. She could not bear to look at him. Dinner had been a miserable, silent affair and she could not wait to get away.

'So you *are* speaking to me; I'm flattered,' he drawled sarcastically. 'I was beginning to wonder, after your stony silence all evening.'

'Answer the question. Anything else you have to say to me can be said through a lawyer,' she flung back, and stepped back as Justin leapt to his feet, knocking his chair over in his haste.

'Zoë, I will not tolerate that kind of talk from you. You are my wife, and my wife you are going to stay. I thought I made that perfectly clear last night.' His black eyes clashed with her contemptuous blue ones. 'But if you want another demonstration I will be happy to oblige.'

'Sex. You think that solves everything.'

'I didn't hear you complaining.'

'Oh! I'm going for the coffee.' And with a toss of her head she walked out of the room and to the kitchen. She knew that Mrs Crumpet was off tonight; she had said goodbye to the lady a few hours earlier, knowing she would not see her again.

Everything was arranged. She had awakened at lunchtime to discover from Mrs Crumpet that Justin had gone to London. She had been glad; the thought of facing him after the night they had spent together had filled her with anger and humiliation.

She had spent the rest of the day quietly and efficiently packing her clothes; the cases were safely stowed in her wardrobe. Her flight was booked on the morning Concorde to New York, and if she could just get through the next few hours without breaking down she would be home free...

'Zoë, we have to talk.' She was just reaching for the coffee-cups from the top shelf of the cupboard and her hand shook at the sound of her husband's voice. 'Here, let me.' He reached over her head and picked up the cups.

She could feel his warm breath on the back of her neck, and slowly, reluctantly, she turned around. Her back was against the kitchen units; Justin was much too close. 'Thank you,' she mumbled, edging warily along the counter and out of his reach.

His long body tensed. 'For God's sake, Zoë, I'm not about to leap on you in the kitchen! There's no need to behave like a frightened rabbit,' he said bitingly. 'Look at me.'

'I'm making the coffee.' She watched the percolator for what seemed like an awfully long time.

'OK, have it your own way. But we will talk.'

She heard the scrape of the pine kitchen chair on the quarry-tile floor and knew that Justin had sat down. She imagined that she could feel his eyes burning into her back and her hand shook when lifting the coffee-jug. She carefully poured the aromatic liquid, filling two cups.

Slowly she turned, a cup in each hand. He was sitting, his elbows on the table, his head in his hands, a dejected slant to his wide shoulders, and for a second she felt a bitter regret for all she had lost. But, as if sensing her scrutiny, he straightened up immediately.

'I'll have my coffee here; it's been a hell of a day in court and I need it,' he said flatly.

'Yes, I'm sure.' They were talking like two strangers—stiltedly, meaninglessly. She placed a cup in front of him and took the seat opposite, and gratefully lifted her own cup to her suddenly parched lips. This was probably the last time she would ever speak to him at any length, she realised, and the thought hurt. Even though she knew it was for the best, she frowned.

'I'm sorry, Zoë.' He looked at her frowning face, his eyes wary. 'I should not have behaved as I did last night. You have every right to be angry——' He broke off and she looked straight at him, her sapphire eyes wide with a hurt she could not disguise.

How could he be so insensitive? He was apologising for making love to her! Not, as she had expected, for marrying her for all the wrong reasons. 'Yes, yes, I damn well have...' She swore furiously.

'It won't happen again, I promise.' He held her gaze, his features taut. 'I—I lost control.'

'You don't see it, do you?' Shaking her head, she stared at him. 'I couldn't give a damn about your control or lack of it.'

'What? Then why?' He contemplated her from beneath half-lowered lids as though her anger were some strange phenomenon.

She drained her cup and stood up. Last night she had not had the nerve to ask about his final betrayal—had not wanted it confirmed—but twenty-four hours and a lot of heart-searching later she had no such qualms.

'Where were you the night before our wedding?' she demanded, and, glancing down, saw the guilty colour rise in his face.

'Janet, was it?' he asked, his mouth turning down. 'I might have guessed.'

'You have not answered the question,' she prompted icily. 'But your face says it all. You spent the night in her apartment until she threw you out at two in the morning.'

'It was not like that,' he said savagely. 'Nothing happened.' He leapt to his feet and, walking around the table, caught her arm as she would have walked out of the door. 'I can explain.' He spun her round to face him. 'If you would just give me the chance.'

Zoë watched him; he looked oddly vulnerable, still wearing the three-piece suit he had worn for the office, but his tie was loose and his hair rumpled. 'Go ahead; it should be interesting,' she sneered.

'I was at Janet's apartment on the eve of our wedding, but you have to understand that I hadn't seen the woman for over six months. She had been on a case in Hong Kong. She returned to England that day and called me. She had heard I was marrying you, and was upset.'

His dark eyes burned down into hers, a rare anxiety in their depths. 'God knows why. I hadn't slept with the woman in over a year. She was a friend, nothing more. I wouldn't have asked you to marry me otherwise, Zoë. Unfortunately Janet seemed to think differently and proceeded to get blind drunk, maudlin and suicidal in that order. I had a terrible time getting away from her.'

She didn't believe him for one second. Justin was a formidable, mature male by any standards; if he wanted to get rid of someone he could with one cutting phrase. He was renowned for it. Never mind about all the rest—his conniving with her uncle, his lack of desire for her when apparently he was a sex maniac with other women. He must think she was a complete fool.

But the worst part was that, deep inside, she wanted to believe him, to swallow her pride and forgive him. She opened her mouth, about to tell him so, when the telephone rang.

'Oh, hell!' Justin swore violently and, letting go of her arm, marched across the kitchen to the wall-mounted telephone and picked up the receiver.

'Yes, Gifford here,' he barked.

But Zoë was glad of the distraction. Without him holding her and the mesmerising quality of his dark gaze muddling her mind she knew what she had to do. Get away... She turned towards the door.

'Zoë.' He called her name. She glanced back over her shoulder; one of his hands was stretched out to her, the other over the mouthpiece. 'Come here.'

Why not? It would be the last time, she told herself, and crossed to his side. He curved his long arm around her waist and hauled her in tight to his body. 'I have to drive back to London. A client has got in a bit of a bind.' He said urgently, 'I'll probably be back very late. I won't disturb you. But we will continue this discussion over breakfast, yes?' His mouth curved into a wary smile. 'Please?'

'Yes,' she affirmed. 'About nine, in the conservatory; the weather forecast is good for tomorrow.' And she would be long gone...

'Fine.' He gave her a relieved look and, bending, pressed a swift, hard kiss on her lips.

She responded—she could not help herself—but she laughed without amusement as she walked upstairs. How could she sink so low? Discuss the weather with an Englishman and he was instantly reassured of one's reliability, she thought wryly, completely ignoring the fact that neither Justin nor she was totally English.

CHAPTER FIVE

THE VIP lounge for the Concorde flight to New York was filling up slowly. Zoë sat in a comfortable, soft-cushioned sofa, her head back and her eyes closed. She had done it; she had left her husband.

It had been ridiculously easy. With her bags already packed, she had simply crept out of the house at the crack of dawn, and free-wheeled her car down the drive so that the noise would not wake Justin.

She had known he was asleep because she had lain awake all night and heard him come home well after three in the morning. She had listened to him enter her room and feigned sleep when he'd stood over her and whispered her name. Much later she had stealthily crossed to his room, and heard the deep, even tenor of his breathing, before slipping quietly away.

'Zoë. What are you doing here?'

The sound of a familiar voice startled her, and her eyes flew open to rest on the rangy figure of the tall Texan as he strolled across the lounge towards her. 'Same as you—catching a plane, I hope.' Her attempt at humour was pathetic, and her smile wobbled dangerous. 'I—I got away earlier than expected,' she added hesitantly.

'And does your husband know?' Wayne asked quietly, sympathy softening his hard face as he lowered his considerable length on to the sofa beside her.

She shook her head, moisture flooding her lovely eyes, too choked to speak.

'Want to tell me about it?' His arm slid comfortingly around her shoulders, and the sheer will-power that had carried her through the past two days finally deserted her. Zoë turned her face into his broad chest and let the tears fall.

Neither of them saw the powerfully built, black-haired man enter the lounge and stop just inside the door; nor did they see the look of devastation in his eyes before he turned and left.

Zoë pulled on her cut-off jeans and slipped a Lycra bandeau around her breasts. She found a large, brightly coloured bath-towel and slung it over her shoulder; she picked up a paperback, and a sun-block cream, then wandered out of the house on to the wide sundeck.

Her gaze swept along the sandy beach; a couple of joggers lifted their hands and waved. She waved back, a tiny smile lighting her huge eyes. She breathed deeply, relishing the scent of sand and the sea, the pacific rollers rhythmically lapping the beach—a soothing music to her trouble mind.

On arriving in America two months ago, she had gratefully accepted Wayne's offer of accommodation at his Malibu beach-house. He had listened to her tearful story of her ill-fated marriage, had comforted her, and in a more practical way had handed over to her the quite substantial amount of money in her trust fund.

She dropped the book and the sun lotion on the table, and the towel on a nearby lounger, before stretching her scantily clad body out on top of it. She had acquired a light tan in the past few weeks, but this was to be her last day in the Californian sun. Tomorrow she was moving to Maine. It was for the best; she had to make a life for herself—she placed a protective hand over her stomach—especially now that she knew she was pregnant.

Wayne was an extremely attractive man, and a true friend, but she had realised very quickly that she did not fit into the free-and-easy, party-going lifestyle that her parents had enjoyed and Wayne still pursued. She had been a teenager when she'd left America; she had returned from England a badly hurt, disillusioned young woman, and somewhere along the way she had fallen between the two lifestyles.

She was luckier than most—she had money—but her own pride and sense of self-worth would not allow her to sit around doing nothing for very long. She had to make a new start.

She liked Wayne, but over the last few weeks she had had a sneaking suspicion that he would not be averse to something more. She was finished with men for good, but she had no desire to lose Wayne's friendship, so, as tactfully as she could, she had told him that she was moving to Maine. Her excuse that the Californian climate was too hot for her he appeared to accept, and anyway she had gone to school in Portland; she loved the area.

Once Wayne had realised that she was serious he had done everything he could to help her. He had flown her up to Portland in his own private jet, and in a whirlwind drive up the coast she had fallen in love with the tiny village of Rowena Cove, situated on a spindly peninsula pointing out into the sea midway between Brunswick and Bath.

She had viewed and signed a lease on a lovely old white-painted, double-fronted eighteenth-century house. Dark green shutters framed windows that looked out over Casco Bay and the clincher for her had been a large, airy attic, fitted out as a studio.

Zoë stretched and yawned widely. The afternoon heat was wonderful but she was too fair to tan easily; she would have to go in shortly. She sat up and hitched up her top. Her clothes were packed and ready; the house

she had leased was part-furnished and even had a daily
housekeeper—a Mrs Bacon from the village—so she
would not be entirely alone.

A shadow darkened her lovely eyes. Not so long ago
she had thought that she would never be alone again;
she had been a fool to herself, loving a ruthless, ambitious man: Justin. Simply thinking of him took all the
sunshine out of the day. It still hurt. She had the horrible conviction that it always would...

Two days ago when the local medical centre had confirmed her pregnancy she had been elated and terrified
in equal proportion. But, once she had recovered from
the initial shock, reaction had set in.

In her heart of hearts she knew she should tell Justin—
he was the father and entitled to know. She had even
considered swallowing her pride and returning to
England to try and make some kind of marriage for the
sake of their unborn child.

But she was no longer the girl who had fled so hastily
from England; she had had time to think, to absorb the
pain of her husband's betrayal. She accepted that Justin
did not, nor ever had loved her, and, thinking clearly
and realistically, she dared not take the risk of returning
to England.

Justin was a powerful man in the judicial system of
the country, a high-flyer with all the right connections.
If he decided he wanted the child and not her, she knew
that if it came to a custody battle, she would not stand
a chance, and she wasn't prepared to take the risk.

'So this is your hide-away.' The deep, melodious voice
echoed on the still air.

For a second she thought she was hallucinating as her
startled gaze fell on the man ascending the steps from
the beach to the deck. Justin here? In California? She
couldn't believe it...

But it was true. He stopped a mere foot away from where she sat frozen in shock. His brown eyes took in every detail of the way she looked—her long blonde hair falling around her face in a tangled mass, the skimpy green band around her full breasts, her cut-off jeans hanging low on her hips. She knew she looked a mess— bare-legged, barefoot and, if he did but know it, pregnant.

A guilty tide of red flooded up her face, but she tilted her chin defiantly and forced herself to withstand his insulting perusal, her own eyes cold as ice. 'A hide-away? I think not... You're here.' She was proud of her steady voice, but she had to clasp her hands together to hide their trembling.

He looked thinner, she thought. His thick black hair curled over the collar of a cream silk shirt, and a leather belt low on his hips supported matching chinos. He needed a haircut, she thought inconsequentially, but nothing could detract from his air of ruthless power nor his vibrant sexuality.

Except herself, she realised sadly, he had never had any trouble controlling his sexy body around her... Which only confirmed what she had been forced to accept when she'd left him. He had never really cared about her.

'Or should I call it a love-nest?' he sneered contemptuously.

'Love-nest?' she parroted, tearing her gaze away from his hard body. What on earth was he talking about? 'Are you off your trolley?'

'I must have been to believe in you, you wanton, adulterous little whore.' His dark eyes flared with rage, his Latin ancestry overcoming his usual, practised British restraint. 'My God! The man is even older than I am, and has apparently been lusting after you since you were a child. It's disgusting.'

Zoë caught her breath, a reciprocal anger flooding her veins. How dared he try to smear her simply to cover his own guilt? But, thinking fast, she guessed where he had got the perverted idea from immediately, and in a cold fury she challenged him.

'Ah! The valentine cards—the last one you claimed you had sent me. But then they do say an honest lawyer is hard to find,' she prompted sarcastically.

'Bitch.' He reached for her, his eyes savage, and for a second she was terrified, but she refused to show it.

Instead, with studied indifference, she arched one delicate eyebrow. 'Really, Justin...it isn't like you to be so unimaginative.'

His hands fell to his sides, his fists clenched, the knuckles gleaming white as he fought to regain his superhuman control, and he won... 'Defending yourself—you have changed,' he ground out between his teeth. 'I take it lover-boy isn't here?'

His dark eyes roamed over her with contempt, demanding a response, but she refused to give him the satisfaction. His face tightening, he watched her in tense, hostile silence for a long, long moment...

Finally a derisory smile curved his hard mouth, and he stepped back. 'Never mind; it's of no importance to me any more,' he said with insulting arrogance. 'I have some papers for you to sign, and then I see no reason why we should ever meet again.'

Zoë wrapped her arms protectively around her body, cold despite the fierce heat of the afternoon sun. She knew he did not love her, but to hear him say he never wanted to see her again was like twisting a knife in her already bleeding heart. The decision was made for her. He would never know she was pregnant. The child would be hers and hers alone, she vowed silently.

As for the rest... That he could be so devious as to try and blame her... To insinuate that she and Wayne...

It was despicable and he wasn't going to get away with it. 'And I see no reason for your presence here in the first place,' she finally retaliated. 'There is such a thing as a mail service.'

'And you would know all about servicing males, my sweet wife,' he mocked silkily. 'Wayne, Nigel and God knows how many more I don't know about.'

Zoë stared at him, deliberately holding his eyes. 'For a man who aspires to be a judge you are singularly lacking in insight.'

'Where you are concerned I would have to agree,' he conceded cynically, his eyes sliding over her with cool insolence, stripping away her brief garments, exposing her naked flesh beneath. Humiliatingly she felt a hardening in her breasts but forced herself not to react.

'I was fooled by your display of innocence, but not any more.' His knowing gaze roamed from the soft swell of her breasts, clearly outlined beneath the fine fabric, up to her flushed face.

'Look at you, and this place.' His glance encompassed the magnificent beach-house and returned to her, his eyes wandering insolently over her yet again. 'You're almost naked, sprawled on a lounger, the archetypal sybarite.'

It was his iron control and his reserve that infuriated her almost as much as his words; only Justin could insult a person so thoroughly without batting an eyelid.

'Forget your fancy language—a lazy, luxury-loving nymphomaniac would have done,' she spat back furiously. She had had enough; she jumped to her feet. 'What did you come for, Justin? I'm not in the mood for games.'

'What are you in the mood for?' he demanded, catching hold of her wrist with sudden violence and pulling her against the hard, male warmth of his body.

She stiffened, instantly aware of his masculine heat, his personal scent. His mouth brushed hers, and she ached to surrender to the longed-for pleasure of his touch. But she refused to give in to her baser urges. That way lay hell! Instead, she jerked her head back and stared up into his calculating eyes.

'Please say what you have to say and leave.' He was much too close, and it took all of her strength to breathe evenly, to control her heavily beating heart.

His eyes darkened. 'I'm not some casual mate you can dismiss with a word,' he grated, tightening his grip on her wrist, and for a moment she felt the force of his rage at her casual dismissal.

'Your fabled control is slipping again, Justin, darling,' she mocked.

'I think not,' he said tightly, his fingers lacing through hers, his thumb stroking the palm of her hand with deliberate provocation. 'But you, Zoë——' his eyes cruelly captured hers as the arm around her waist moved lightly over her near-naked back in a deliberately arousing caress '—you never could say no,' he taunted silkily.

She took a deep, shuddering breath. She had been stupid to bait him. 'I've learnt.'

'Shall we test that?' Justin suggested huskily, but Zoë was too quick for him, and, freeing herself from his grasp, she put the lounger between them.

'No. Our marriage is over; we have nothing more to say to each other.' And for good measure she added, 'And Wayne will be back very soon.'

At the mention of Wayne Justin straightened and stared at her, his hard body taut. Then his dark eyes closed briefly, and when he opened them the cold bleakness of his gaze made her shiver. 'You're right of course. Let's get down to business. I have the papers in my car. I won't be a minute.'

She watched as he strode down the steps, and a shaft of pain lanced through her. In a few minutes she would sign the divorce papers. She looked around the sun-kissed beach, at the gentle sway of the ocean, her eyes misting with tears. She dashed her hand across her eyes. She would not cry.

Slipping into the house, she hastily pulled a large, baggy shirt over her trembling body and fastened the buttons to her neck before returning to the deck.

She watched Justin walk towards her with a briefcase in one hand; he placed it on the table and sprung the lock.

'There was no need to cover up for me. I have seen it all before,' he remarked, casually eyeing the over-long shirt. 'I can't say I admire your lover's taste in shirts.'

Actually it was her own shirt—one she wore when painting. She opened her mouth to say so and closed it again. Let him think she had a lover—what did it matter? 'Just give me the divorce papers and tell me where to sign.'

'Divorce? Oh, no, Zoë. I'm not making it that easy for you.'

Their eyes met and held and her heart lurched in her breast. Was it possible that he wanted her back? 'Then why are you here?' she asked quietly.

He laughed without humour. 'What do you think? That I want you back?' His too intelligent brain had read her mind. 'You were good in bed, but not that good, and I don't go in for used goods, my dear. But I am your guardian until you're twenty-five.'

She had forgotten all about Uncle Bertie's will. 'But under the circumstances surely——?'

Justin cut in, 'Exactly. I see no reason to continue the guardianship.' He spread some papers on the table. 'If you will read these and sign where indicated. You'll find Black Gables is to be sold at a decent price and after probate all the monies accruing to you will be placed in a bank of your choice. Any further communication between us can be conducted by your American lawyer.'

Justin the lawyer was in total control as he raised cold eyes to her face. 'I'll take a walk while you read the relevant documents, and if you have any questions I'll be more than happy to answer them.'

She could not believe what she was hearing. 'And why no divorce?' She was not aware that she had asked the question out loud.

'I have a career to think of. There is no way I will divorce you, and as you have no grounds for divorcing me you must wait the five years as set down in English law.'

She could feel the anger welling up inside her. She had no grounds? The arrogance of the man was incredible. 'You bastard,' she said softly, shaking her head. How had she ever thought she loved such a man?

Snatching the papers from the table, she didn't bother reading them, but simply signed where indicated and thrust them back at him. 'Now get out.'

Leaving him standing, she dashed back into the house, sliding the glass doors closed behind her.

Zoë drove slowly along the main street of Rowena Cove and up the hill leading out of the village. She turned left into a drive leading towards the sea and parked outside the dark green door of her home. For a long moment she simply sat behind the wheel of her practical, four-wheel-drive Range Rover and stared out across the cold waters of the bay.

Three and a half years ago, when she had moved to this house at the top of the hill, she had fallen in love with the place. It was true that in the summer mid-coast Maine was flooded with visitors, but at this time of year—a crisp day in March—the locals had Rowena Cove pretty much to themselves.

Her mind went back to the first winter, and the birth of her son. A fierce snowstorm had blocked the roads out of the village and her beloved boy had been born at home with the help of a local sailor's wife, Margy. Since that day they had become firm friends. Two years ago they had gone into business together, running a small gift shop specialising in hand-painted cards. Amazingly the business had flourished. In the summer they designed Christmas cards, in the fall, valentine cards.

She choked back a sob. Val, her son, loved playing with Margy's daughter Tessa—or he had until his illness had prevented him. She glanced distractedly around the yard. A magpie landed on a tree-stump and was speedily joined by another one. One for sorrow, two for joy... A bitterly ironic smile twisted her lips. There was no mirth, no laughter any more, and she no longer believed in omens.

Her son had been born fit and healthy at twelve-thirty on the morning of Valentine's day. She had called him Valentine after checking the meaning in the baby book. Derived from the Latin, meaning strong, powerful, healthy... The last was the cruellest cut of all.

She glanced over her shoulder at her son, belted into the back seat and fast asleep. His beautiful black curls fell over his forehead, his long lashes, so like his father's, rested on the curve of his cheek, and she was stricken with pain and guilt.

She opened the car door and got out. The cottage door was open and Mrs Bacon was standing on the step, a worried frown creasing her already lined face.

'You're days late; is everything all right?'

Zoë simply shook her head and, opening the rear door, leant in and lifted the sleeping boy into her arms. She hugged him close, burrowing her face in his sweet-smelling hair; he was so precious that she could not bear to lose him, and she was not going to. She would go anywhere, do anything, sacrifice everything she owned, but her son would live, she vowed silently. Straightening her back, a grim determination in her stride, she walked into the hall.

'I'm putting him straight to bed, Mrs B,' she murmured as she passed the older woman and headed for the stairs.

An hour later, bathed and changed into a soft blue jogging-suit, she took a last peek at her sleeping son, dropped a soft kiss on his tousled head, and went back downstairs. In the kitchen Mrs B was waiting, a pot of tea at the ready.

Zoë collapsed on the ladder-backed chair at the pine table and, zombie-like, took the cup Mrs B offered, and seconds later she was greedily drinking the refreshing brew. She didn't have to speak—her face said it all. Devoid of make-up, white as a sheet, her eyes circled in purple shadows, she was a picture of devastation.

'You know what's wrong?' Mrs B prompted quietly.

'Yes, and I still can't accept it,' she said almost to herself. 'It's too incredible for words. Why us?' The cry was from her heart.

The housekeeper shook her head, the sympathy in her hazel eyes plain to see.

'At Christmas Val was a healthy boy—maybe a little tired, but I thought it was simply the aftermath of the cold he had earlier. When he started pre-school in January, I thought maybe that was what was tiring him out.

'I took him to Dr Bell——' she lifted red-rimmed eyes to her companion '—you know I did, and he gave him junior vitamins and a blood test. Then he said he was anaemic.

'I took him to Portland and then to New York University Hospital; he had blood transfusions, but still he was anaemic. Last week we stayed in hospital together while they carried out further investigations. So where did I go wrong? What else could I have done?'

'Don't blame yourself, Zoë; you have done everything you could.'

Zoë straightened in the chair. 'It's odd—money never meant very much to me, probably because I always had enough. I can pay the best in the world to treat my son, and it isn't going to do a damn bit of good.' She thumped her fist on the table in an agony of frustration. 'It is so unfair...'

Mrs B caught her hand in hers. 'Steady, girl,' she soothed gently. 'Tell me what's wrong.'

Zoë threw back her head, laughing, on the edge of hysteria. 'You won't believe it; I didn't at first. I thought it was some kind of sick joke. My son, my baby Val, has apparently got Fanconi's anaemia.

'Before you say anything, I know it sounds like an Italian pizza house. It would be funny if it wasn't so serious.' And, dropping her arms on the table, she laid her head on them and wept...

She didn't hear the doorbell, or the murmur of voices in the corridor; she was too lost in her own despair.

'Hey, come on, partner.' A pudgy arm reached around her shoulders, and she lifted her head to meet the soft brown eyes of Margy.

'Margy, has Mrs B told you?'

'Yes, and nothing is as bad as it seems, believe me, I know. Medical science is a miraculous thing, as is the power of prayer. Pull yourself together. Where is the fighting spirit, the human dynamo that has made our business a success? Use the same energy and determination and you and Val will beat this together.'

'You're right, I know, but sometimes, just sometimes, the strength goes——'

'More tea?' Mrs B cut in. 'Because if not, and you don't want anything else, I need to get home.'

'No, thanks, Mrs B, and thank you for being here today. I'm truly grateful,' Zoë said quietly.

Five minutes later the two friends retired to the living-room, where Mrs B had left a welcoming log fire burning, and, after opening a bottle of wine, they relaxed in the comfortable armchairs.

Zoë quietly sipped the wine and gazed into the red-gold flames, trying to sort her thoughts into some kind of order. She could do nothing about the churning in her stomach; it was plain anxiety, and likely to be with her for evermore.

'So what exactly did Professor Barnet say?'

She raised her head, her blue eyes gazing over Margy's dark head, the sweet, rounded face full of sympathy and understanding, and thanked God that she had such a good friend.

'I saw him the day we arrived, and then the team took over and carried out all kinds of investigations on Val. I had another appointment to see Professor Barnet and hear the results, but when I walked into his consulting rooms it was a Dr Freda Lark, his replacement; apparently he was involved in a pile-up on the freeway the night before and suffering from concussion.'

She took a sip of her wine. 'It was weird but, in a way, probably better. She hadn't had time to read the file thoroughly. So she gave it to me straight. Val is suffering from Fanconi's anaemia.'

She took another swallow of wine, her eyes meeting Margy's. 'I know—I'd never heard of it either. Apparently it's extremely rare; they were not sure what causes it, but the treatment——'

She stopped and swallowed the lump in her throat, determined not to cry again.

'The treatment is transfusions, which Val has already had, followed by, in twelve days' time, a course of chemotherapy.' Just the word horrified her; she licked her dry lips, 'And the best chance for success is a bone-marrow transplant.'

'Oh, God! Does Val know—understand?'

'Yes, and sort of,' Zoë said sadly. 'The reason we were late back was that I was screened immediately and I waited for the result to see if it matched.' She drained her glass and, picking up the bottle, refilled it. 'I don't.' A despairing sigh escaped her as she handed the bottle to her friend.

Margy took the bottle but put it on the floor. 'You must tell him; you have no choice.'

Zoë knew she was not referring to Val. She had confided the circumstances of her marriage and separation to Margy years ago.

'I know... Dr Lark, unaware of my marital state, was quite adamant. ''Bring your husband in as soon as possible and any brothers and sisters; the most likely match is the immediate family.''' Dully Zoë repeated the doctor's words, but not all of them... The rest she was keeping to herself...

'There is the phone.' Margy indicated the instrument on the table with a wave of her hand. 'Call him now, Zoë.'

'Ring Justin? Just like that? No, I can't.'

'Why? Are you frightened he won't come? Doesn't he like children?'

Zoë thought for a moment, remembering her years in England, which had been mostly happy if she was honest with herself.

'Truthfully, I don't really know. He did suggest that we wait a year before having any of our own. But then

Justin was very good to me when I was a teenager. In fact, when I think about it, he did tell me the reason he stayed late in London every Monday night was that he taught boxing at a boys' club. He got a blue at Oxford for boxing. And, before you ask, I have no idea why it's a *blue*.'

'There you are, then! He must like kids. Ring the man.'

Zoë twirled the stem of her glass around her fingers. 'Actually, I thought if you didn't mind, Margy...' She glanced across at her friend. 'I know it's an imposition, but I wondered if you would do me an enormous favour.'

'If you want me to ask him, forget it. This is something you have to do yourself.'

'No, no, nothing like that.' A brief smile lifted the corners of her mouth but quickly vanished. 'I wondered if you would look after Val for the weekend. Much as I hate to leave him for any time at all, I thought I'd fly to England on Friday and ask Justin in person, and hopefully bring him back with me on Monday.

'I know it's a lot to ask, but you're the only person I trust to look after Val. He loves Tessa...' She was pleading, but it was so vitally important.

Margy dashed across to her and wrapped her arms around her, hugging her tightly. 'Yes, of course. What are friends for? And don't worry about a thing. Take the plane and catch the man. Hog-tie him if you have to but get him back here.'

CHAPTER SIX

Zoë brushed a stray tendril of damp hair from her brow and glanced around the crowded airport, panic building in her chest. Was she doing the right thing? Did she have a choice? They were calling her flight for London; this was it...

She did not notice the admiring glances of the male passengers as she walked across the tarmac to the waiting Concorde. Her silver-blonde hair, scraped back in a ponytail, bounced between her shoulder-blades as she walked. She was dressed in a smart wool suit of pale cream and khaki tweed. The jacket fell, loosely sculptured, over a plain cream waistcoat and khaki silk shirt; the short, straight skirt fitted snugly over her slim hips and ended an inch above her knees. High-heeled, matching shoes flattered her shapely legs and added to her petite height of five feet.

She had the face of an angel, and a figure men would die for, but it wasn't just sex appeal that she possessed; there was something in her face, in the shadows lurking in the sapphire-blue eyes—a deep-rooted sadness that made every man within range want to comfort and protect her.

Zoë would have been horrified if she had known the impression she created. Ever since her twenty-first birthday and the break-up of her marriage she had decided that she had to harden up or she was going to be an exceptionally vulnerable person.

She thought she had succeeded and living in America had helped. In a country where women were proud of their independence and determination she had found it easier to adjust to being a single mother, to balancing family with an interesting career at no loss to either.

She removed her jacket, folded it neatly over the back of her seat and sat down. She placed her shoulder-bag on the floor in front of her and, dropping her head back against the cushion, closed her eyes.

The past few months had tested her character to the limit, but her steely determination had never wavered. She was like a lioness with her cub—she would do anything to protect her most cherished possession, her son Val, and if that meant leaving him for a few days to seek out his father so be it... Even though she was already missing Val dreadfully.

She was unaware of the elderly gentleman who sat down beside her, only opening her eyes when the voice of the stewardess broke into her reverie.

'Would you like a drink, madam?'

'No, thank you.' She tried to smile. 'And please don't disturb me for the rest of the flight. I don't want to eat, I simply want to rest. OK?'

The girl gave her a peculiar look. 'Certainly, madam. Have a nice flight.'

Zoë sighed and, turning her head to the window, closed her eyes again, her mind a seething mass of troubled thoughts. In a handful of hours—with luck—she would be face to face with Justin once again. The thought was frightening, but what she had set out to do absolutely terrified her...

She went over in her head one more time her conversation with Dr Lark. She had not dared tell Margy the whole story, sure that she would disapprove. Dr Lark was a wife and mother herself, and, after confirming that the immediate family was the best bet for a bone-marrow donation, she had elaborated on the theme.

'So long as you love children, and if there is no medical reason why you can't have more, then, if you want to give your son every chance available, and if you are prepared to explore every avenue open to you, I suggest you and your husband get you pregnant as quickly as possible. The long-term prognosis for your son is not good, but a baby as young as a one or two can donate bone marrow. I know if I was in your position I wouldn't hesitate.'

She knew Professor Barnet would never have suggested such a course of action because he knew her marital status. But Dr Lark, unaware of the true state of Zoë's marriage, had had no such reservations.

She shifted restlessly in her seat. The girl who had fled England at twenty-one would never have attempted to seduce her imposing husband, but the woman Zoë had become over the intervening years was determined to do just that...

She had debated the morality of her intention over a clutch of sleepless nights until her head had spun. She was still not absolutely sure that she was doing the right thing, but her mind was made up, and deep down inside she consoled herself with the knowledge that she would love another child.

She didn't know if Justin was involved with another woman and she didn't really care. All she cared about was getting him into bed at the first possible moment—and not necessarily a bed.

Luckily the next few days were the optimum time for her to conceive, and she was taking no chances. She guessed that once she told him about Val his rage at her deceit in hiding his son from him, and his contempt for her, would make any chance she had of seducing him virtually nil. That was why she had no intention of telling him until after she had done her utmost to get him into bed. After all—she rationalised her decision—Justin had used her. Now it was her turn to use him . . .

The warning-lights instructing passengers to fasten their seatbelts flashed on, and minutes later the aeroplane touched down at Heathrow Airport.

Once through Customs, she picked up her suitcase and marched briskly out of the building and into a waiting taxi. She had booked in advance at the Savoy, and an hour later she was sitting on the bed in her hotel room, the telephone in her hand.

Her first set-back came when she dialled Justin's chambers in the Inner Temple and to her astonishment discovered that he no longer worked there.

She chewed her bottom lip, deep in thought. Apparently her estranged husband was now a well-known international company lawyer with offices in a highly prestigious block in the heart of the city. What had happened to make him change his career plan? she wondered uneasily.

But, dismissing the troublesome thought, she glanced at the number she had been given, and dialled it. Another set-back—Justin was not in his office, and was not expected back that day.

She glanced at her watch. Fool—she'd forgotten to set it forward and it was almost six in the evening. She made one more call, long-distance to Margy in Rowena's Cove. Five minutes later, with her son's 'I love you, Mom,' ringing in her ears, she brushed the moisture from her eyes and with a renewed sense of urgency and determination stripped off her clothes and quickly washed and changed.

It was a very different woman who stepped into a taxi at the hotel entrance and gave the address of Justin's apartment. A fine jersey wool dress, the exact colour of her astonishing blue eyes, clung to every curve of her body. The simple cross-over-style bodice revealed a shadowy cleavage and fastened with two buttons at her waist; the skirt, a wrap-over that revealed an enticing glimpse of leg when she moved, ended just above her knee.

Her make-up was light but carefully applied to hide the purple smudges of worry under her eyes that marred her otherwise perfect complexion. She had left her long pale blonde hair loose, simply clipped back behind each ear with two pearl-trimmed combs. A tantalising scent added to the sophisticated image, along with a fake fur jacket draped elegantly across her shoulders.

She was dressed for seduction; braless, her only underwear was briefs and a garter belt—mere wisps of cream silk lace—and the finest silk stockings. Navy shoes with four-inch heels and a matching shoulder-bag completed her outfit.

She nervously clutched her bag and her stomach sank as the lift whooshed her up to the fourth floor of the mansion block where Justin had his apartment. She stepped out of the lift and walked to the door, taking a deep breath, and, with a quick pat of her hair, rang the bell.

The woman who answered the door was beautiful, Zoë thought dismally. She was tall and elegant, with long black hair falling in a mass of curls over her shoulders, huge, thick-lashed, dark eyes, and a complexion the colour of golden honey. Suddenly Zoë hoped desperately that Justin *had* moved apartment. A man with a woman like this waiting for him was hardly likely to be sidetracked by a petite blonde.

'Yes, can I help you?' Even the voice was a husky purr.

'I was looking for Justin Gifford; he used to live here. But perhaps he has moved?' she asked hopefully. She knew she was no competition for this stunning woman.

'No, you have the right address.' The woman's eyes narrowed in puzzlement on Zoë's pale face. 'Are you a colleague of his? You look vaguely familiar.'

'Yes—yes, I am.' She jumped at the excuse; she could not give up at the first hurdle—her son's life might depend on it.

'In that case, if it's important, you'd better come in and wait; I'm expecting him back any minute.'

Grasping the strap of her shoulder-bag as if it were a lifeline, Zoë had never been more aware of her diminutive stature as she followed the elegant back of the gorgeous woman down a short hall and into a large living-room. Her hope of seducing Justin was looking more unlikely by the minute. Perhaps she would do better just to tell him about Val and trust to his good nature to do the right thing.

The woman called over her shoulder as she crossed to a drinks cabinet, 'I didn't catch your name.'

'Zoë. Zoë Gifford,' she murmured, glancing around the elegant room. A huge, curved black hide sofa was placed in front of an open fire with two large wing-back chairs set at either side of it. The only new addition she noticed was an exquisite Chinese rug in shades of pink and gold that broke the uniformity of the wall-to-wall beige carpet.

'My God, you've got some nerve, you bitch!'

Zoë's head shot up at the loud exclamation, startled by the venom in the woman's voice. 'Pardon me?'

'Don't come the innocent act with me. You destroyed Justin once and there is no way I will allow you to repeat the exercise.'

'I destroyed...?' she cried in amazement. Who the hell did this woman think she was talking to? The pain at the break-up of her marriage, the worry and torment over her son all coalesced together in one great, frustrating fury. She shot her a scathing glance. 'I don't know who you are, and I don't want to know. But——'

'Leave now before I——'

'Jess, what's all the yelling . . . ?'

Slowly Zoë turned towards the door, her heart in her mouth; she would have known that voice anywhere. Justin . . . Heaven knew she had heard it in her dreams, cried the name in her sleep a thousand times!

But the grim-faced stranger standing less than two feet distant, towering head and shoulders over her, was not the man she remembered. The night-black hair was liberally sprinkled with grey, the brown eyes cautiously hooded and hard in a harsh face, the grooves bracketing his mouth deeper, the lips thinner, denoting years of iron control.

'Zoë?' He drawled her name enquiringly.

She stood frozen like a statue before him, simply because her legs were incapable of movement. He was watching her, waiting for her to speak. She swallowed painfully and, gripping the strap of her shoulder-bag so tightly that her nails dug into her palms, raised her eyes to his. 'Hello, Justin,' she managed, her voice high and nervous.

'This is a surprise. To what do I owe the honour?' he asked cynically.

'Justin, get her out of here. You don't want to talk to her.' Jess spoke before Zoë could form a reply.

'Jess, I believe you have a lecture to attend. I suggest you leave. I am perfectly capable of handling the situation without any help from you.'

Zoë almost felt sorry for the other woman. Justin at his commanding, arrogant best was a formidable adversary, as she knew to her cost. When she had first run away to America she had been hurt and angry, but after his denouement of her character and morals at their last meeting in California her anger had turned to hatred.

She was here now for her son, and him alone. Otherwise she would not have willingly put herself within a million miles of Justin Gifford.

'Don't say I didn't warn you.' The woman shot a vitriolic glance at Zoë before storming out of the room, and some moments later Zoë jumped at the sound of the front door slamming.

'You will have to excuse Jess—she's very protective,' Justin said smoothly, before closing the space between them. 'And forgets her manners sometimes. Allow me.' His hands fell on her shoulders. She stiffened in instant rejection to his touch.

'Your jacket,' he prompted silkily, and slid the fake fur from her shoulders, his gaze flickering slowly over her slender curves, then sliding back to settle on her wide, wary blue eyes.

'Very nice, if a little slim,' he opined coolly.

Her eyes sparkled with resentment, but she dared not retaliate. She was here for a purpose. 'Thank you,' she said in a low voice.

He inclined his black head in acknowledgement and walked past her across the room to a drinks cabinet. He turned and glanced back at her. 'A drink? Whisky, brandy? You look as if you could use one.' His dark gaze raked over her from head to foot and back to her pale face.

'For heaven's sake sit down,' he said harshly, with the first show of emotion he had revealed since seeing her, and she realised that he was not as in control as he appeared. 'You look as if you're going to take flight at any second, yet you must have a purpose in being here.'

'Thank you,' she said inanely yet again. Her brain seemed to have stopped working. She forced her legs to carry her to the hide sofa, and sank on to it with relief. Seeing him again had reawakened all the old pain, the bitter sense of betrayal, and she knew she shouldn't have come.

Margy had been right. She should have simply called him from America, explained the circumstances and trusted to his compassion and better nature. Obviously he had a woman living with him—a very beautiful woman—and her idea of seducing him into, she hoped, making her pregnant before revealing the existence of Val hadn't a hope in hell of succeeding.

She briefly closed her eyes. But she was still going to try; it was a ridiculous long shot, but no sacrifice was too great for her son. She lifted her head, a determined gleam in her sapphire eyes, and found Justin standing in front of her, holding a glass of amber liquid in his hand.

'Thank you yet again,' she said easily, and took the glass, raised it to her lips, and swallowed it down. It burnt her throat and hit her empty stomach like a fire ball. She coughed and spluttered, the glass wavering precariously in her grasp.

He took it from her hand and smacked her on the back with some force. 'That was twenty-year-old cognac, meant to be savoured, not sloshed down like water,' he informed her drily, lowering his muscular length down beside her on the sofa.

'I realise that now,' she said curtly when her coughing fit had subsided enough for her to speak. She glanced sideways at him. He had changed—he was leaner and harder, she thought. But considering that he was now almost forty he looked remarkably good. But then he had been a mature male when she had met him whereas she had been a girl. She knew she had changed more than he had; from twenty-one to nearly twenty-five was a big jump from a girl to a mature woman and mother.

He was wearing an immaculately tailored grey pin-stripe suit, a white shirt and a silk tie in muted grey stripes—conservative to his fingertips. But it did not stop the powerful force of his sexuality hitting her just as hard as it had all those years ago the first time she had seen him. The old, familiar ache in her stomach, the rapid rise of her pulse—nothing had changed.

Justin had stopped patting her back, but whether by accident or design his long arm lay along the back of the sofa almost but not quite touching her shoulders; for a second she was tempted to relax back against him and pour out her desperate fear for their son.

'So, Zoë——' his smile was sardonic '—what are you doing here? I can't believe it's because you finally missed me,' he drawled cynically.

'No. I was passing through London and I thought it might be nice to look you up. I called your chambers and they said you had left.' She forgot her own troubles for a moment, intrigued to know what had happened to her husband in the past few years. 'Why, Justin? I thought you were all set to become a judge.'

'I seem to remember you thought a lot of things about me, Zoë—none of them true, and I find your presence here today incredible to say the least.' His aura of hospitality vanished in a flash. His dark eyes narrowed assessingly on her small face. 'Cut the old pals act, Zoë, and give me the real reason for your visit,' he commanded arrogantly. 'I'm a busy man; I have no time for games.'

'Perhaps I thought we could be friends—we were once,' she said lightly. She could hardly blurt out that she had hated him for the past four years, she thought wryly, especially when she was planning on getting him into bed.

'You want to be my friend?' His eyes hardened. 'Now, why, I wonder, do I find that so difficult to believe?' He smiled at her mockingly over the rim of his glass and she felt a wave of heat surge up her cheeks. Deceit did not come easily to her.

'I know my appearing out of the blue like this must be a shock to you,' she offered. Gathering her scattered wits about her, she made a concentrated effort to disarm him. She turned slightly towards him and, fixing him with her dazzling blue eyes, continued, 'But in the past few years I have grown and matured a little, I hope, and it seems pointless for the two of us to be enemies.'

She forced a casual smile and deliberately lowered her tone. 'We did share a lot together.' She lifted one shoulder languidly against the beautiful blue jersey, exaggerating her cleavage. She saw his eyes flick down to her breasts and quickly away, and her heart leapt; she was getting to him, she knew.

'We had some fun,' she went on. Her knee brushed his thigh and she felt him tense. Heady with success, she ploughed on. 'And I'm sure Uncle Bertie would turn in his grave if he knew his two favourite people couldn't even speak to each other.'

She felt guilty using her uncle but desperate need called for desperate measures, and nothing was sacred in the fight for her son's life.

'Interesting and succinctly argued, my dear Zoë. You have grown up.' His arrogant glance trailed from the silky main of pale blonde hair down to where the low V of her dress exposed the tantalising curve of her firm breasts. 'I find I rather like the idea of you and me as friends—much more civilised,' he opined, with a hint of mocking amusement in his deep brown eyes.

'Yes, yes, it is,' she agreed, grateful for his easy compliance while not questioning it. His arm around the back of the sofa fell to her shoulders, and her stomach tightened in revulsion at his touch. Or was it revulsion?

'Good, I'm glad we agree, and it is good to see you.' He smiled lazily. 'It must be almost four years—we have a lot to catch up on.' Idly his long fingers massaged her shoulder, but her reaction was anything but idle. She tensed as she felt the old familiar ache ignite deep inside her, and his thigh brushing hers made her catch her breath.

'You must tell me what you've been doing with yourself.' His hand slid down to her arm. 'You've obviously lost weight—you were always slender, but now you're almost gaunt.'

'It's the fashion,' she muttered, angry with herself for her total inability to remain immune to the man's sensual charm. Hadn't she learnt her lesson in their ill-fated marriage? She was there for a purpose—a chance to save her son's life—and she would do whatever she had to, but no way was she falling under Justin's spell again. Once was more than enough.

'Whatever.' He shrugged dismissively. 'You still look good and I'm not pressed for time tonight; give me five minutes to shower and change and I'll take you out to dinner.'

'Out to dinner' was not what she had in mind—a crowded restaurant would not help her plan at all. 'There's no need to take me out,' she demurred. 'You must have had a long day. Why not show me the kitchen and I'll rustle up an omelette or something?'

Justin stood up. 'What a very obliging woman you have turned out to be, Zoë.' A sardonic gleam of amusement flashed down at her and, clasping her hand, he pulled her to her feet. 'You still wear your wedding-ring,' he noted abruptly, turning her left hand over in his.

Zoë glanced up at him, her sapphire eyes catching his, and she trembled at the flash of some undefined emotion in their dark depths and tried to pull away. His grasp tightened for a moment as if he would detain her, his gaze oddly intent on her lovely face, then suddenly she was free.

'I wouldn't dream of allowing you to mar your soft hands with anything so mundane as cooking,' he drawled. 'My housekeeper will have prepared something. Help yourself to another drink. I won't be a moment.'

She watched his departure with mixed feelings. Her plan was going well. But why was Justin being so obliging? She had fully expected to have to battle her way into his company. Instead he had almost immediately invited her to dinner. Strange!

Uneasily she crossed to the drinks cabinet and helped herself to a small cognac. She needed it... She sipped the fiery liquid, her confidence slowly rising. No! Not so strange, she told herself firmly. After all, they were both mature, sophisticated adults. Well, Justin certainly was, she amended wryly, making her way back to the sofa and sitting down. She wasn't half so sure about herself...

She smoothed the skirt of her dress over her thighs with a trembling hand. What could be more natural than two adults sharing a dinner? And if it led to something more then that was perfectly acceptable, she told herself staunchly. She wasn't a child, and she had slept with Justin countless times...

She drained the glass and placed it on a nearby table. The hair on the back of her neck prickled and she looked up as the man occupying her thoughts walked in, a bottle of champagne in one hand and two glasses in the other.

'Quite like old times—my wife waiting for me.' His dark eyes roamed leisurely over her reclining figure with a blatant sensual insolence that made her feel as if he had stripped her naked.

She fought down the slow flush spreading through her body at his scrutiny, her confidence dipping alarmingly and a feeling of helplessness overtaking her as she stared at him. He had obviously showered and changed. Huge and casually dressed in a soft blue shirt and jeans, with a black lambswool sweater draped elegantly over his broad shoulders, his black hair damp and curling on his brow, he looked years younger and his likeness to Val was heartbreaking.

She swallowed nervously, looking away. Why was it that of all the men in the world Justin was the only one to make her heart race and her nerves quiver? It wasn't fair. Bitterness rose like gall in her throat; she should hate him that he was so vibrantly male, so *alive*, and her precious child...

No, she must not think negative thoughts, she reprimanded herself, and glanced back at Justin. He was watching her, waiting... His dark, steady gaze was so like Val's that she was hit by an overwhelming sense of guilt.

He placed the glasses on the table and finally his deep voice broke the long silence. 'A toast, I thought—to celebrate.' He deftly opened the champagne; the cork popped and bounced off the ceiling, the foaming liquid spurted from the bottle, but quickly the two glasses were filled, and he lowered his long body down beside her on the sofa. 'We can be friends! Isn't that right?' he questioned silkily.

She shied away nervously; there was something about him that she couldn't put a finger on. And his smile, as he handed her a glass of champagne, didn't quite reach his eyes.

'A toast. To old friends, hmm?'

The words were polite, even banal. Justin appeared relaxed, affable, but beneath his sophisticated exterior she had an odd premonition that something dark and dangerous lurked. Her fingers brushed his as she took the glass, an electric sensation shooting up her arm. She flinched.

'Careful, Zoë,' he prompted, his free hand closing over her wrist. 'Allow me.' In an intimate gesture he urged her hand holding the glass to her mouth while he lifted his own glass. His dark eyes caught and held hers. 'To a civilised friendship, my dear.'

She tensed. His face, only inches from hers, was playing havoc with her veneer of sophisticated control, and she was sure that he must be able to sense it. So, with a calm she was far from feeling, she placed her small hand on his arm, her expression beguiling. 'To a long and civilised friendship,' she responded sweetly, and took a healthy sip of the champagne.

There was nothing civilised about the murderous rage leaping in her companion's eyes, but, luckily for Zoë, she never saw it. By the time she was brave enough to face him again he had finished his drink, his large frame sprawled back on the sofa, a lazy smile in his brown eyes.

'So tell me, what have you been doing with yourself the last few years? You don't have much of a tan for a Californian.'

'Oh, I don't live in California!' she exclaimed, glad to get on to a neutral topic. 'I have a house in Maine, in a lovely little fishing village. Actually, the area is rather like England——'

'Could be why it's known as New England,' he interrupted with a mocking grin.

Her answering smile was completely spontaneous, and for the next few hours she felt as if she had stepped back in time. Over a delicious if simple dinner of a typically English dish—hotpot—he was a charming, witty host.

'Not your nouvelle cuisine,' he said wryly as he carried a tray with a coffee-pot and two cups into the living-room, where Zoë was already relaxing once again on the sofa. 'But ideal for a cold March day.'

The coffee finished, Zoë, sipping a glass of cognac, allowed her eyes to roam over Justin. He was lounging back beside her, his long legs stretched out before him; she noted the stretched denim over his muscular thighs and—whether it was the wine or the food or simply because she was feeling relaxed for the first time in weeks she wasn't sure—a sharp tug of sexual awareness lanced painfully through her.

'You never did tell me why you changed careers,' she blurted, taking another drink of her cognac—anything to get her mind away from the slight friction of his thigh against her own, the overt sensuality of the man. Forgetting for the moment that she was supposed to be seducing him, she suddenly realised that he had skilfully discovered all about her home and career, and a couple of times she had almost slipped up and mentioned Val. But he had revealed very little about himself.

She glanced back at him. He was gazing down at his drink, idly twisting the glass between his long fingers, his expression hidden from her.

'I don't think I was ever cut out to be a judge—as you so rightly told me the last time we met.'

'Oh, but...'

'Don't worry.' His hand slid casually to rest on her thigh, and he squeezed it reassuringly. Except that, to Zoë, it was not reassuring—quite the opposite: intensely arousing. 'It had nothing to do with you. For years I went along with what Bertie wanted for me simply because he had been good to me and I wanted to please him. But I realised a few months after his death that it was his ambition I was following, not my own. So I went back to international law.'

'Do you like it?' she asked breathlessly; his hand, idly stroking her thigh, was playing havoc with her nervous system.

'I love it. I get to travel; I make vast amounts of money.'

Then she remembered Janet; he had once worked with the woman in that field. She tensed. 'And I suppose you work with Janet again?'

'Good God, no!' he exclaimed, easing up, his arm somehow finding its way around her shoulder. 'She put herself in a clinic and dried out and then married Bob. They have two children.'

'Dried out?' she queried.

'Surely you knew the woman was an alcoholic? Everyone else did.'

She had a vivid image of Janet drinking from the champagne bottle at her twenty-first, and the thought that she had allowed Janet's drunken revelations to persuade her to run out on Justin was oddly disturbing, but, banishing her unease, she responded.

'I never guessed. But Janet—with a family—the mind boggles.' She grinned, inexplicably lighter of heart.

'Is it so strange for a woman to want a home and family, Zoë? Are you really such a determined career girl? The girl I married was longing to have a baby. I often wondered—if I hadn't insisted on waiting a year— if I had made you pregnant—would you have run away so easily?'

The colour drained from her face. He was getting too near the truth, and she lowered her eyes, unable to meet his dark, enquiring gaze. The anger, the hatred and bitterness she had felt because he had married her but never loved her were no excuse for what she had done. She was flooded with guilt and remorse and combined with too much liquor it was a lethal combination.

She opened her mouth to tell him about Val, but before she could confess Justin continued, 'Jess and I debated the point once. She's of the opinion that a child only makes a bad relationship worse. I'm not so sure.'

The mention of Jess acted like a bucket of cold water over Zoë, reminding her exactly why she was here, and time was running out if her plan was to work. His girlfriend might be back any minute.

'Yes, well, it is all rather academic now,' she said lightly, and, turning towards him, she deliberately placed her small hand on his chest. She tilted her head back to look up into his harshly attractive face.

'Don't let's talk about the past. I'm much more interested in the present.' And, forcing a regretful smile to her lips and widening her blue eyes appealingly, she added, 'I'm glad we can be friends, Justin.'

She inched her hand higher to where the top buttons of his shirt were open to reveal the strong line of his throat. Her fingers grazed his skin and she felt him tense. 'It is rather late; Jess will be back soon.' She was fishing, but she needed to know. 'I'd better get back to my hotel.'

His dark eyes glittered dangerously down into hers as he caught her hand and held it trapped against his chest. 'Jess won't be back tonight, and you don't have to go— you can stay here.'

He lifted her hand to his mouth, his lips kissing her fingertips, his eyes coolly assessing on her upturned face. 'You understand that I'm not into celibacy?' The corners of his hard mouth quirked in a sensuous smile. 'If that's going to be a problem for you, say so. I will understand,' he said smoothly.

She understood all right. He was offering her what she had set out to get. It was there in the flare of desire in his eyes, quickly masked by his hooded lids. He sucked one of her fingers into his mouth and she trembled, her pulse galloping.

He was still the only man who could arouse the sensual side of her nature. His touch still had the power to turn her will to mush. It was galling to admit. It left a bitter sense of self-loathing in her troubled conscience but it didn't make it any the less true.

She should have been ecstatic but instead all she felt was a profound sadness. This man had been the love of her life, and he had confirmed what she had always known. He was a man who betrayed the women in his life without a qualm.

'But Jess...' She needed to hear him confirm his duplicity. It would help to ease her own sense of guilt.

'Don't worry your head about Jess. She's a woman of the world, Zoë, the same as you.' And, lifting her on to his lap, he bent to her mouth.

Much later she was to wonder if she had actually seduced her husband, or if it had been the other way around...

CHAPTER SEVEN

ZOË had imagined that she would have to force herself to accept Justin's lovemaking, to tell herself it was for her son's life and just lie back and think of England!

But at the first touch of his lips on hers she knew that she had lied to herself for years. She was swamped with emotions—feelings so intense that they stole the breath from her body and moisture stung her eyes.

He'd never kissed her in quite that way before. She felt the soft touch of his mouth, the gentle nibble of his teeth against her lips, the lick of his tongue teasingly soothing the supposed bite, savouring the taste of her.

'So lush, so soft,' he breathed against her lips. 'Open your mouth for me, Zoë,' he husked, his lips rubbing sensually against hers, taunting her into sharing the pleasure, and she did . . .

Before, he had always been a silent lover, but now he had no such reservations, and his deep, throaty murmurings, interspersed with longer and deeper kisses, were her downfall—hot, damp heat filled her loins and she felt it burn through her whole body.

As she was held on his lap her arms, of their own volition, wound around his neck; her mouth followed where his led. The husky male scent of him surrounded and seduced her; she felt the rigid muscles of his thighs beneath her and she pressed into his hard body with hungry need.

'No,' he whispered roughly. 'Not here.' Rising to his feet, with Zoë held firmly in his arms, his breathing quick and unsteady, he strode through the apartment. He

111

shouldered open the bedroom door, and kicked it shut
with his foot, not stopping until he was standing next
to the king-size bed.

She looked searchingly up into the dark eyes so close
to her own. 'Justin, I . . .' She wanted some reassurance,
perhaps, that it wasn't simply a physical thing.

'It's too late, Zoë. I'm too old for teasing games; I
want you badly. Now!' he said harshly.

She trembled with fear or frustration—she didn't know
which. 'Yes,' she murmured. It didn't really matter
which! She had to go through with it for Val—but also,
her own innate sense of honesty forced her to admit, for
herself... She had had nearly four long years of celibacy
and she had never stopped wanting Justin, however much
she had tried to deny it.

She sighed, a deep, shuddering breath, as Justin stood
her on her feet and quickly unbuttoned her dress, slipping
it from her shoulders to pool in a heap on the floor.

'Nice,' he growled, his hungry eyes slanting over her
near-naked form, the proud tilt of her full breasts, and
the wisp of lace briefs cupping her feminine curls.

The urge to cover herself was compelling but juvenile.
Justin had seen her naked countless times in the past,
but it didn't stop her feeling helplessly exposed. Running
her tongue nervously over dry lips, she forced herself to
stand immobile, her arms at her sides; she couldn't afford
to let him see her nervousness.

And he didn't. His dark eyes glittered as they followed the tip of her tongue, while the fingers of one
hand hooked in her briefs and pulled them down. His
gaze lowered lazily over her naked body and then,
dropping to his knees, he slowly unfastened her sus-
penders and trailed her stockings down her legs, and
finally he glanced up at her and undid her garter belt.
His large hands curved around her waist and he brushed
her stomach with his lips. Her body jerked in instant

reaction, and she bit her lip to prevent herself crying out.

Justin rose to his feet and simply stared at her. 'I thought the first time I unwrapped my Valentine girl in this room that you were perfect.' He shook his dark head wonderingly.

She raised her eyes to his. And I thought you loved me, she wanted to cry, but didn't. In those days she had believed that love made the world go round. A brief, ironic smile flitted across her softly flushed face. With maturity had come realism. Now she accepted that it was simple thermodynamics...

They stared at each other, the air around them crackling with tension. He divested himself of his own clothes, never taking his eyes off her, drinking in the sight of her pale skin, the soft, full curve of her breasts, the secret, downy hair.

But Zoë was doing some observing of her own. 'Justin.' She breathed his name. Awed all over again by his superbly muscled form, which was naked and glowing golden in the dim light of one small lamp, she had forgotten how splendidly male, how powerful he was.

Then he lowered his head and pressed his mouth to the valley between her breasts. His hands curving around and down over her buttocks, he pulled her hard against him. His mouth trailed up her throat, and his dark eyes gleamed with a feral light in the semi-darkness.

'Remember that night, Zoë? The night you promised to be mine?' he demanded, a sharp edge to his deep voice. 'My own personal valentine.'

It was cruel of him to remind her—as if she could ever forget. She had imagined that it was a lucky omen, getting engaged on Valentine's day, but life had taught her differently. She slid her arms up around his neck and swayed against him.

'Forget the past and let's enjoy tonight,' she pleaded. For once she wanted to forget all her troubles, all the heartache, and surrender herself to the mindless pleasure that only he could give her. Tomorrow she would count the cost, but now now!

'Enjoy the sex; I take it you are protected?'

'Yes,' she lied.

'Of course, my wanton little wife.' His mouth covered hers again, but this time with passionate insistence.

She felt the need in him; her legs trembled against his, her stomach quivered against his hard, masculine life force, and she opened her mouth, her tongue twining with his. He pulled back sharply.

'Slowly, slowly, my darling.' Dazed by his kisses, she did not hear the sneer in his voice. 'It should be interesting discovering what you've learnt over the years,' he drawled with a cynicism that was lost on her as he swung her once more in his arms and deposited them both on the bed.

He looked down the length of her. 'You're as beautiful as ever.' His hand closed over her breasts. 'But before you were a girl; now you are a woman.' His thumb grazed the tip of her breast. 'A surprisingly voluptuous woman in some areas.' His head bent and as his mouth sucked the rosy peak she arched up towards him, fire shooting from her breast to her loins.

'You still like that?' He lifted his head to stare at her, his brown eyes glittering with sensual desire in the harsh contours of his handsome face. She met his eyes, her own wide and dazed with emotion.

'You know I do,' she whispered, her hands lifting to shape his wide shoulders, flow down his strong arms, and move to the broad expanse of his hairy chest. 'I like anything you do,' she confessed throatily, and, like a sculptor moulding a work of art, she traced his masculine form, her fingers delighting in remembering the satin-smooth feel of his skin. Her hands stretched to his waist and around over his firm buttocks.

'Zoë,' he growled, and leant down, his mouth lightly brushing her lips and then finding her breast once more. She lifted her hands and buried them in the thick, silky hair of his head, holding him against her as, arching, she offered him her aching breasts. She shuddered as his hot, moist mouth fed on one swollen nipple and then the other, until a strangled cry escaped her.

The touch of his tongue and the caress of his hand as it stroked seductively down her body, his long inquisitive fingers tangling in the bush of blonde curls at her thighs and pulling, gently teasing, before they slid deftly into the soft, feminine folds of her most secret flesh, were almost more than she could bear.

She was spinning out of control to a hot, healing place where nothing mattered but the pleasure he could give her and she could give him. His mouth followed the trail of his hands and she exulted in the hard rasp of his chin against her tender flesh, his seeking fingers that found every pleasure-point with unerring accuracy, the hard pressure of his mighty body.

She traced the length of his spine, her small hand curving around the firm male buttock, seeking the hard core of him, but suddenly he grasped her wrist and pushed her hand away, rolling on to his back.

'Not yet. Slow down,' he rasped urgently.

But Zoë ignored him; she was consumed by a burning urgency. Perhaps subconsciously she knew this was all she would have of him; tomorrow would bring grim reality, but tonight was hers.

She felt as though she had been in an emotional prison for years and had finally broken free. She followed him over, sprawling across his sweat-wet body, her long hair a tangled mass spread across his shoulders as her mouth found the male, pebble-like nipples buried deep in the soft, curling chest hair. She moved restlessly against him, her hands shaping his thighs as her teeth bit the tiny buds.

'God, Zoë, what are you doing to me?' Justin groaned and, grasping her around the waist, he lifted her slightly.

She raised her head and looked down into glittering black eyes, her own unfocused. She felt him shaking beneath her, then suddenly he lifted her higher and lowered her sharply down, impaling her with his male strength. She cried out as he filled her, her slender body clenching around him in convulsive need.

He raised his head and, catching the tip of her breast with his teeth, sucked the hard nipple into the dark cavern of his mouth with the same rhythm as he surged into her pulsating flesh. She heard his harsh moan as she recognised her own whimpering cries. Every nerve, every sinew in her body pulled tight with an excruciating tension. She battled to breathe, then her body convulsed in a rapturous fulfilment, the ecstasy prolonged as Justin increased the tempo to explode inside her.

'Zoë.' He rasped her name and held her hard down, his fingers digging into the flesh of her waist as his great body bucked uncontrollably beneath her in a shattering climax.

She fell against his chest; she felt his arms close around her; she heard the rapid pounding of his powerful heart beneath her ear, her own body twitching in the aftermath of love.

Some time later she didn't hear Justin's huskily voiced question, 'Are you OK?' She was asleep.

It was a long, dark tunnel. Water seeped from the arched roof and trickled down the rough stone walls to sink into the soil, turning the ground to mud. She was cold to the bone and terrified.

Then, in the distance, at the end of the tunnel, outlined in a silver glow, stood two figures. Zoë moved towards them, slowly, sluggishly, the mud holding her back. She saw them smile and her blue eyes widened to their fullest extent as she recognised them, her face radiant with joy. Justin and Val.

She tried to hurry, but as she stretched out her hand towards them the figures turned and she froze in horror as the boy vanished, disappearing into the man.

'No, no. Valentine!' she screamed.

'Zoë, Zoë, wake up.'

Her eyes flew open, the horror of the dream reflected in the blue depths. For a moment she was totally disorientated. But the large body looming over her and the hand on her head, smoothing her hair from her brow, were real.

'You were having a bad dream.'

'Justin,' she murmured, reality returning. She lifted her hand and outlined his square jaw, the slant of his cheekbones. He was warm and alive and in bed with her. But Val... God, no! She refused to see it as another omen. She was finished with superstition. It solved nothing.

He caught her hand and pressed it to his lips. 'I know I'm no oil-painting——' his dark eyes gleamed with ironic amusement '—but I can honestly say that you're the only woman I've driven into having a nightmare. I would never have mentioned our first night together if I had known it would cause such a violent reaction. Are you all right?'

She moved her hand around the back of his neck, her fingers tangling in his night-black hair. He hadn't guessed her secret, and she wasn't going to tell him. Not yet... She needed him tonight...

'More than all right,' she responded huskily, urging his head down and pressing her lips against his smiling mouth while her other hand found its way around his hard thigh.

Zoë leant up on one elbow. Careful not to disturb the sleeping man, she let her gaze wander over his rugged face, the softly curling hair. In sleep, Justin looked years younger and so like Val that it brought tears to her eyes. They had made love countless times—two healthy adults glorying in each other's body. She ached all over, but the biggest ache was in her heart. She could pretend to herself no longer. She loved Justin—always had and probably always would.

With the added maturity that the years and her worry over her son had given her she knew that if she had the last few years to live over again, she would never have left Justin. The only reality in life was the family. She had allowed stupid, girlish pride to wreck hers, and she had to bear the guilt for it.

She should never have let a drunken woman's ramblings, or the fact that her uncle had only been trying to do what he thought was best for her, break up her marriage. Nor should she have allowed Justin to think that Wayne was her lover because of childish tit-for-tat jealousy.

She should have stayed with him and fought for his love. It would not have changed the fact that their son was ill, but at least Val would have had the support of a father as well as herself over the past few terrifying months.

As the early morning sun splintered through the window, outshining the single lamp's gold glow, she made a momentous decision. She was going to swallow her pride and confess everything—tell Justin she loved him and beg his forgiveness for hiding his son from him, and, hopefully, they could go forward into the future, supporting each other and better able to face the trials to come.

She sighed contentedly, her decision made, and, wriggling down beneath the covers, put her arm around Justin's waist and snuggled up against his large, warm body. For the first time in ages she felt safe, protected and no longer alone with her worries, and, yawning widely, she fell into a deep, dreamless sleep.

Zoë stirred, opening her eyes lazily; the seductive scent of freshly ground coffee lingered in the air. She stretched out a hand but she was alone in the wide bed. Justin must be up making the coffee, she thought, a small smug smile lighting her eyes as the events of the previous night flickered through her mind. She hauled herself into a sitting position, and, flicking the tumbled mass of her blonde hair from her eyes, looked up.

'Good, you're awake.'

'Justin.' He was standing by the bed, naked except for a small towel carelessly tied around his hips, and the memory of the intimacies they had so recently shared made her blush scarlet. It was stupid, she knew, but she felt inexplicably shy.

He leant forward and he felt her heartbeat accelerate, sure that he was going to kiss her, but instead he placed a cup of coffee on the bedside table and straightened up.

'Thank you,' she murmured huskily, vitally aware of his imposing presence and the glitter in his eyes as they roamed over her flushed face. She felt her nipples harden as his gaze dropped lower. She was naked from the waist up and her first reaction was to pull the sheet up, but, with her decision of the early hours of the morning fresh in her mind, she didn't. She was an adult woman and this was her husband . . .

'Very nice,' he drawled mockingly, 'but I haven't time this morning; drink your coffee and get dressed. I'll drop you off at your hotel on the way to the gym.'

'There's no need. I'm quite happy to stay here until you get back,' she replied with a nonchalance she did not feel. She couldn't really blame him for suggesting the hotel. She had given him no reason to believe differently.

She pulled the cover up over her breasts and, bravely raising her eyes to his, added firmly, 'We need to talk, Justin.' She had been a coward once, but never again. 'I have a confession to make; it's important and after last night——' she had been going to say, I realise I love you, but she never got to finish the sentence.

'Last night was a one-off, Zoë,' he cut in ruthlessly. 'Good fun, but I'm not a fool. I know exactly why you were so willing to leap into bed with me.'

'But you can't...' This wasn't going at all as she had envisaged. She stared up at him, unable to fathom the brooding look in his dark eyes. 'I only realised myself...'

'I do read the gossip columns occasionally.'

'Gossip columns?' What on earth was he talking about?

'Cut out the innocent act, sweetheart,' he bit out. 'I've been expecting you for weeks—ever since lover-boy Wayne got himself engaged to a starlet. What happened? Get tired of you, did he?' he queried coldly. 'Or perhaps tired of waiting for you to be free?'

His black eyes narrowed angrily. 'My God, you have some nerve, I'll give you that. Did you really think you could walk back into my life when Wayne dropped you and expect me to take you back? Was that what your pathetic attempt at seducing me last night was all about?'

She flinched under his tirade, not really following his reasoning. 'No, it's not true,' she whispered, too stunned by his total misreading of the situation even to argue.

She grasped the sheet tighter around her suddenly cold body.

'"No, it's not true."' He viciously mimicked her feeble denial. 'That's your trouble, Zoë; you wouldn't know the truth if it got up and smacked you in the face. You never did, as you proved conclusively years ago when you ran out on me.'

'Please, Justin, you have to listen to me.' She swung her feet to the floor and stood up, the sheet draped haphazardly around her body. He caught her by the shoulders and held her away from him, but she swayed towards him, the urgency in her expression undeniable. 'I know I was wrong before, but I realised last night that I love you, and I——'

His fingers dug into her flesh for a second and then he flung her away from him with such force that she fell back across the bed, his fury hitting her like a blast from the devil's own fiery furnace.

'You bitch! You don't know the meaning of the word, and I've wasted enough time already this morning. I'm sick of your games. Get dressed and get out.' And, swinging on his heel, he flung out of the bedroom.

Zoë watched him leave, her eyes filling with tears. She brushed them away with the back of her hand and got up off the bed. She had done her crying over Justin years ago and nothing had changed. What had she expected?

Nothing, her common sense told her. A big fat zero... Wasn't that why she'd decided to get him into bed without telling him about Val? Because she knew, had always known, that he didn't give a damn for her? But he would be furious when he found out about Val.

Then she remembered Jess. The woman was probably due back any minute. Last night, in a sensuous haze, she had lost her wits completely. How could she have forgotten Justin's luscious girlfriend? But in the clear light of day the reality of her situation rushed in on her.

Quickly she washed and dressed and went looking for him. He had said that he was sick of games and that was good enough for her. She had no more time to waste. She found him in the kitchen; he was leaning casually against the kitchen bench, drinking a cup of coffee. He looked up as she entered, his dark eyes as cold and remote as a polar icecap.

'You took my advice, I see.' He glanced over her slight figure. She was dressed in her stylish clothes of last night but minus her make-up, and her hair was ruthlessly pulled back and fastened with an elastic band.

'Yes, but before I go I have something to show you.' Sitting down at the kitchen table, she opened her bag and, rummaging around, withdrew a snapshot and held it out to him. 'This is Val, our son—the reason I'm here.' She saw no point in softening the blow; Justin didn't deserve her consideration. When had he ever considered her?

He stepped towards her and took the proffered picture, glanced at it, and as she watched she saw him stiffen. 'I only have your word for that; this child could be any man's,' he said, cynicism icing his voice. 'I seem to remember you and I always took precautions. What kind of an idiot do you take me for, Zoë? Discovered how wealthy I am now, is that it?'

It was lucky that she was already sitting down because otherwise, at his denial of her child, she would certainly have collapsed. She had thought that she had covered every eventuality, but it had never crossed her mind that he would query his part in the parenting. She stared up at him through a mist of pain and rising anger which she did not attempt to hide.

'No, it's not your money I need, it's you. Val is three years old; he was conceived the night of Uncle Bertie's funeral. If you remember, it was the one time in our brief marriage you actually spent the night with me, and we did have unprotected sex.'

She caught a glimpse of shocked horror on his handsome face, but she didn't care if she hurt him. 'You're a lawyer.' Her mouth twisted in a bitter grimace. 'If you insist I'll agree to a DNA test to confirm the parenting, but it will have to be quick.'

He was caught and he knew it, but he was obviously not ecstatic at the thought of a child; his granite-hard features showed no flicker of emotion. She briefly closed her eyes, her head drooping on the slender column of her neck, her son, her ever present worry, swamping her mind.

'You knew you were pregnant when you left me,' Justin prompted stonily, and, pulling out a chair, sat down opposite her.

Zoë, her head bent, studying her clasped hands, either didn't hear or ignored his comment. 'He was born the following February—Valentine's day—hence his name.'

She was back in the past, a reminiscent smile softening her blue eyes. 'He was a beautiful baby, and it's stupid, I know, but I remember hearing this country and western singer on the radio. It was a song about a boy called Sue. He had given his son that name because he wasn't going to be around to look after him, and I thought, what with the day and all, Val was really very appropriate.'

Long fingers caught her chin, their pressure hard as Justin forced her head back until he could look into her face. She recoiled at the blistering fury leaping in his eyes.

'You knew—if not in England, in California.' The words came out harsh and clipped.

'Knew what?' She had not been listening to him.

His thumb and finger dug into her throat and she gasped at the pain. 'You knew you were pregnant the last time I saw you. Didn't you...? Didn't you?' he demanded harshly, his rugged face livid with rage. 'You could have told me, you cruel little bitch,' he snarled.

She forced herself to stay cool, though inside she was trembling in fear at the force of his rage. He got to his feet and she could sense the threat of violence in his hard body as he leant over the table, breathing down on her hapless head. 'You're hurting my neck.' She gulped.

His hand fell away and he was around the table in seconds. 'Tell me... I need to know.' His long fingers gripped her shoulders, digging into her flesh. 'What did I ever do to make you hate me?' he demanded tautly, his iron self-control slowly reasserting itself. 'Why? Why do you hate me so much you would deny me my own child?'

She was puzzled, not so much by his anger—she had expected that—but by the hesitation, the hint of pain in his usually authoritarian tone. 'I was going to tell you, but you said you never wanted to see me again. There didn't seem much point,' she said brittlely.

Justin briefly closed his eyes, and she could have sworn that she saw his wide shoulders shudder. His hands squeezed her shoulders; she glanced up at his face and their eyes met.

'God forgive you, Zoë, because I don't think I ever will,' he said with a finality that was chilling. But, worse, she recognised a look of such torment in the depth of his deep brown eyes that she was struck dumb.

'Where is he now? I want to see him. Does he know I'm his father? Thank God I didn't give you the divorce you wanted. He is legally my child, and you've cheated me out of three years of his life. Well, not any more, Zoë.'

He was making her head spin with his questions, his comments, and she couldn't think straight. But he never let up.

'I intend to fight you for him. I'll challenge you through every court both here and in the States. I want my son, Zoë. I will have him.' His lips twisted in a satanic smile. 'I will win, I promise you, and once I get him I intend to keep him...'

His words were cutting into her heart like a knife, and she couldn't stand any more. She had been battling to control her tumultuous emotions for far too long.

'Keep him? Keep him?' she cried. 'You fool, you don't understand. I would gladly give him to you this very second if only it would make him well.' Her eyes wild, she screamed, 'Val is ill—very, very ill. Why the hell do you think I'm here now? Do you think I enjoy leaving him with Margy while I trek halfway around the world seeking his father?' She was blinded by fury and fear, and, shrugging off his restraining hands, she leapt to her feet.

He was towering over her, large and intimidating, but she was beyond worrying about his threat. 'I would never have set foot in your home in a million years if it weren't for my son. But he needs you; you are almost his last chance, and I would sup with the devil if I had to, to save him.'

The tears filled her eyes but she dashed them away with the back of her hand. 'In this case, that happens to be you.'

She spun on her heel, not sure where she was going, but she was pulled back roughly into his arms and lifted completely off her feet.

'What the hell do you mean?' He looked down into her tempestuous little face. 'Ill?'

That was how Jess found them.

'My God! Justin, you didn't spend the night with her? How could you?'

Zoë felt his sudden tension as he slowly lowered her down the length of his hard body until her feet found the floor. She pushed herself out of his arms, red with embarrassment. His mistress was back... Her glance went to the tall, elegant woman and then to Justin's harsh face.

'You don't understand, Jess.'

The tender light in his eyes as he spoke to the other woman was enough for Zoë. She had to get out of there and fast.

'Understand? You're a fool, Justin.' She cast a disparaging glance at Zoë's tiny, dishevelled figure. 'You've always been a pushover for her. Will you never learn?'

'Not now, Jess,' he said tersely. 'Just leave. Please.'

Zoë picked up her bag from the table and began edging towards the door. She had done what she set out to do; it was up to Justin now. But she couldn't bear to be the third wheel in a lovers' quarrel; she hadn't the stomach for it.

'Zoë, where the hell do you think you're going?' Justin demanded, just as she was slipping out of the door and into the hall.

She stopped. 'I need to get back to my hotel; I need a bath, a change of clothes.'

She might have been tiny but she had an inner core of pure steel, and she had never needed it more than at this moment. She could not blame Jess for her fury; she felt dirty herself. But if the other woman's dagger looks were meant to unnerve her they would not succeed. Too much was at stake.

Zoë ploughed on bravely with her mission regardless. She firmly told Justin her room number. 'Call me when you're free. I'll be there until Monday.'

His black head tilted to one side and he studied her pale face with a chilling implacability. 'You're in no fit state to go anywhere by yourself, and I don't trust you not to disappear.'

'Disappear?' A glimmer of a smile twisted her lips, Margy's admonition ringing in her mind: 'Hog-tie him if you have to'. 'I can promise you there is no fear of that,' she said with a touch of irony. 'I'll be in all weekend waiting for your call——'

'Really, Justin, you're not going to fall for that?' Jess interrupted. 'You're far too intelligent.'

'Shut up, Jess.' Justin walked past her to Zoë, and, curling his fingers around the top of her arm, glanced back over his shoulder at his mistress. 'I'll call you later.' He looked down at Zoë. 'I'll give you a lift to your hotel.'

Zoë swallowed at the remote look on his darkly attractive face, and, with a brief nod of her fair head, she agreed.

She felt drained of all emotion as she walked with Justin through the underground car park to where a sleek black Jaguar was waiting. He handed her into the front seat and slid in beside her.

She watched him deftly manoeuvre the car out into the Saturday morning traffic with enviable ease. One hand rested lightly on the gear lever; the long fingers of his other hand curved delicately around the leather-bound steering-wheel.

She had a vivid image of those same fingers on her naked flesh last night and her pulse leapt with remembered pleasure.

He really was an incredibly sexy man, she thought, glancing sideways at his hard profile. Unfortunately he was completely lacking in morals where women were concerned. It was just as well, she acknowledged with dry irony, or she would never have ended up in his bed last night.

She sighed and stared out of the window. It was raining, the sky a dull, leaden grey and an accurate reflection of her state of mind. She sighed again.

'Valentine,' Justin drawled. 'What kind of name is that for my son?' He glanced at her, his face cold and expressionless. 'Though I shouldn't be surprised; you always were a fey, whimsical kind of child.'

She made no response, and they drove in a lengthening, tense silence that did not improve when they reached the Savoy.

'Get out,' Justin ordered curtly, and before she had gathered herself sufficiently to open the door and slide out he was around the car and taking her arm in a vice-like grip. He passed the car keys to the valet and hustled her into the foyer as if she were an errant child.

When he demanded her room key from Reception, she tried to object. 'There is——'

'Shut up.' He was in a furious temper beneath his controlled exterior, and he flung her into the lift as if she were a rag doll.

But it was no more than she had expected, she thought with stoical resignation.

CHAPTER EIGHT

ANY hope of her ordeal being over quickly was squashed as Justin, granite-faced, pushed her into her own suite and closed the door behind him.

He came towards her. 'Now talk,' he commanded arrogantly. 'And you'd better make it good. I want to know everything about my son, and what you've done with him.' His hands dropped to her narrow shoulders and he stood staring down at her, his black eyes burning on her. 'I've had it with you, Zoë; you've gone too far this time.'

For once the dynamic, powerful Justin had lost his poise; her revelations had clearly knocked him for six. But it gave her no joy. She had thought that after the night they had spent together . . . her realisation that she still loved him . . .

How naïve could one get? She shook her head in disbelief at her own folly. The arrival of Jess had shown Zoë just how degrading her position was. Justin wanted nothing from her but his son.

She drew on her last reserves of strength, determined to concentrate strictly on Val's welfare, and, wiping her own shame and humiliation from her mind, looked Justin straight in the eye and said flatly, 'Please let me go. I need the bathroom, and, in any case, what I have to tell you can't be discussed in a rage.'

She was a mother first and foremost and she refused to discuss her precious son in anger. Too much was at stake and it was vital that she win Justin's support.

A cruel smile smile curved his lips; he caught her face between his hands and pressed his mouth hard down on hers in a savage parody of a kiss, declaring his power and domination.

She swayed, her legs trembling, when he released her. 'Why?' Her tongue licked her swollen lips.

'A reminder!' he said tightly. 'I'll order coffee, but don't keep me waiting too long.'

Ten minutes later Zoë reluctantly walked back into the sitting-room. She had taken the time to have a quick shower and change into a pair of well-washed jeans and a baggy black sweatshirt. Barefoot, with her small face scrubbed clean and her pale, silky hair dragged back and fastened with a blue silk scarf, she had no idea how ridiculously young and vulnerable she looked.

A grim smile touched Justin's mouth when he saw her. His hand shook as he ran it through his thick hair. 'You look so damned innocent. How the hell do you do it?'

'Cursing me will solve nothing,' she said, her blue eyes flickering over him. He was perched on the edge of his chair, a coffee-jug and cups untouched on the table in front of him. She knew she had hurt him badly by denying him his son, but recriminations could come later. First, she needed to explain and get him back to the States with her.

She sat down on the chair opposite his and, leaning forward, filled two cups with the thick, dark brew. Automatically adding one spoonful of sugar to his, she handed it across to him.

'You remembered how I like my coffee; pity you couldn't have remembered to tell me I had a son as easily,' he said with biting sarcasm.

'Please, Justin. Let me tell you in my own way.'

'I can't wait.' His formidable, dark face looked grim. 'It should be interesting. It's not every day that a man is so spectacularly betrayed by his own wife.'

'I never wanted——'

'Cut the excuses, for God's sake! And give it to me straight.' His sensuous mouth curved contemptuously. 'That is, if your devious little mind can grasp the concept.'

She bowed her head, unable to face the banked-down rage in his dark eyes, and began to speak. 'Val is a beautiful little boy—a real live wire, full of curiosity for life, and he looks very like you.

'But last fall I noticed he was much quieter than usual; at first I put it down to the bad weather at the time.' A dry chuckle escaped her. 'My English half blaming everything on the weather, I expect.'

She glanced across at Justin and for a second she faltered, deterred by the unforgiving hardness of his expression.

She swallowed. 'He caught a cold. The doctor gave him antibiotics, and he seemed to recover, but not properly. After Christmas when he started pre-school he still wasn't a hundred per cent. The doctor took a blood test, and confirmed he was anaemic, but when, after vitamins and iron, he was still no better there were further tests.'

Her bottom lip trembled and she had to take a deep, steadying breath before she could go on. Reliving the past desperate weeks and exposing her pain to another person was one of the hardest things she had ever done.

'Go on,' Justin prompted implacably.

'We took a trip to the hospital in Portland; the consultant there recommended a transfer to New York University Hospital and a world-renowned consultant in the field, Professor Barnet. More transfusions, more tests, until a week ago they finally came up with the answer—Fanconi's anaemia, a very rare disease.'

She said the hated words by rote; it was the only way she could deal with the enormity of what had happened to her beloved boy.

'Cause not known. Treatment—a week on Monday Val starts a course of chemotherapy. Ideal solution—a bone-marrow transplant. The problem is that I've been screened and I'm not a match for him.'

Only then did she lift her head.

Justin had gone white about the mouth and his features had settled into a rigid, impenetrable mask, which made what she had to ask him a hundred times harder.

'I'm hoping you will be,' she said, her blue eyes huge and pleading in the unnatural pallor of her small face. 'It's not hard, Justin, believe me. A simple blood test, and, if you match, the transplant is a breeze—honestly,' she insisted urgently. 'A simple operation to extract the marrow from the base of your spine. Two nights in hospital—three at most; nothing worse than a backache.'

'Stop! Stop right there,' he commanded flatly. 'First, have you consulted the best medical opinion available?'

For the next half-hour Zoë was treated to a ruthless cross-examination, Justin's decisive yet politely impersonal questions beating down on her until she wanted to scream and finally did...

'But will you do it?' she cried. 'I have your seat booked on Concorde on Monday. Please simply say yes.'

'God! Need you ask?' Disgust made his lip curl and she squirmed at the contempt in his black gaze as he added, 'Yes, of course.'

Her head fell back against the soft cushion and she closed her eyes. 'Oh, thank God. Thank God!' The relief was tremendous. She had hoped that Justin would do the right thing, but she had never been sure. It was as if the weight of the world lifted from her shoulders. She opened her eyes and looked at him. 'You'll never know how much this means to me, Justin.'

'I think I can guess; he is my son as well,' he returned drily. Getting to his feet and turning on his heel, he strode across to the telephone. He dialled a number and, holding the receiver to his ear, turned and leant against the table, watching her with cold dark eyes, his long lashes flicking against his high cheekbones. 'There's no need to wait until Monday. We'll leave today.'

'But——'

He stopped her with a wave of his hand, and she listened in rising amazement as he instructed the unseen person at the other end of the telephone wire to have the jet standing by.

'How?' She seemed to be incapable of stringing two words together.'

His mouth curved sardonically. 'Easy, Zoë,' he said, coming towards her. 'I am a very powerful man in my own way.' He reached down and lifted her up out of the chair as if she weighed no more than a feather, his hands firmly around her tiny waist. 'But I certainly underestimated you, my dear wife,' he drawled harshly. 'Last night had nothing to do with Wayne Sutton, had it?'

She blushed fiery red as he set her on her feet, but kept a firm hold on her. 'No,' she mumbled; could he possibly have guessed? It was one thing to ask an estranged husband to donate bone marrow; it was quite another to try and get oneself pregnant by the same man, especially knowing he had a very lovely 'significant other' in his life.

'You have good reason to look ashamed,' he said with icy disdain, and, grasping her chin, he tilted her scarlet face back the better to see her. 'You deliberately let me do anything I wanted with your sexy little body last night in the hope of softening me up before telling me about my son.'

Now was the moment to tell him the truth—all of it. 'It . . .' She bit her lip.

'You're little better than a whore, but then I always knew that.'

She looked up sharply, meeting his contemptuous gaze with angry eyes. 'It wasn't like that,' she objected.

'Your reason was noble,' he admitted in a deadly quiet voice, 'But don't ever try to barter sex with me again. I will not be used that way. I prefer to do my own hunting.'

A dull foreboding made her shiver; if he ever discovered just how much she had tried to use him he would kill her... 'I wouldn't dream of it,' she said quickly, keeping a wary eye on him.

He smiled—a slow, wicked curve of his hard lips. 'Good,' he murmured, his arm tightening around her waist. His black head bent and his warm mouth fastened on hers in a long, sensuous kiss that made her heart thud in her breast.

She caught her breath as he pushed her away, staring up at him, bewildered and vaguely angry. 'Why did you do that?' she demanded shakily.

'You looked like you needed it, and I sure as hell did,' he grated. 'Now for the sixty-four-thousand-dollar question. What have you told our son about me?' The demand was curt, his dark face taut with resentment. 'If anything.'

Zoë had been expecting the question, but it still did not make answering him any easier. 'You have to understand—Val is very young, and, well, Margy my friend's daughter Tessa is his best friend. Margy's husband was a sailor and he was lost at sea in a round-the-world yacht race.'

'You told him I was dead...?' he rasped.

'No, no, I'm trying to explain. Val only asked once about his father. I told him you were a very important lawyer working thousands of miles away across the sea, but one day he would meet you. I thought...' Actually she hadn't thought very clearly at all; in the back of her mind she had simply thought, One day. But not yet . . .

'Don't bother, Zoë, I can read you like a book. After the five-year separation a quiet divorce and only then any mention of the child. I suppose I should be grateful he even knows I exist, but under the circumstances I don't feel particularly grateful. Call him. Now. I want to speak to him.'

Zoë glanced at her wristwatch. It would be early morning in Rowena Cove. Crossing to the telephone, she placed the call.

Within seconds she was speaking to Margy and, after exchanging the usual greetings, her friend demanded bluntly, 'Have you got him, Zoë?'

'Yes, yes, I have, and he would like to speak to Val. Can you put him on, please?'

'Hi, Mom. When are you coming back? Have you got me a present?' At the sound of her son's childish chatter Zoë's eyes misted with tears.

'Slow down, darling. I'll be home tomorrow and yes, I am bringing you a present.' Sensing Justin's presence behind her, she glanced over her shoulder. His dark eyes burnt implacably into hers as he mouthed the words Tell him, while Val's shout of joy and demands to know what it was rang in her ear. 'I'm bringing your daddy home with me; he's here now and would like to say hello!'

Numbly she handed the receiver to Justin, and watched silently as he spoke to his son for the first time. She choked back a sob, amazed to see his eyes luminous with tears. Only then did the full enormity of what she had done by denying him his son sink into her tired brain, and the feeling of guilt was crushing.

'Here. He wants to say goodbye.' The receiver was pushed back into her hand and she managed to pull herself together enough to finish the call.

She replaced the receiver, her hand shaking, the ecstatic delight in her son's voice ringing in her ears. Val sounded happier than she had heard him in months, and it only added to her own self-disgust.

'I suppose I should thank you, but I don't damn well feel like it! That was my son—my boy.' His angry words flayed her like a whip. 'And you only told me because you were desperate.'

He was right and she bowed her head in shame.

'Oh, for God's sake go! Go and have a rest and then pack. I'll be back in couple of hours. I have a few things to sort out—people to see—before we leave.' He was all brutal efficiency and she should have been glad. Instead she watched him walk out of the suite with a pounding heart and her thoughts in chaos.

They arrived in New York in the early evening, and before Zoë had time to catch her breath they were on another private flight out to Brunswick. Justin had done his homework well, and as he deftly swung the rental car off the interstate at her direction and along the small road that ran to Rowena Cove she could sense the tension mounting in his large body.

She glanced sideways at his grim profile, etched in the lights of a passing car, and her own fear seemed to lessen slightly when she thought of what he had to face.

'Is this it?' The car ground to a halt outside the front door of the cottage.

'Yes.'

'Nice, but hardly your style,' he murmured, following her up the porch steps, his travel bag in one hand, hers in the other. He glanced up at the comfortable-looking old house and then around the headland to the sea beyond.

She made no response as she fiddled in her bag for the door key; finding it, she opened the door, walked into the hall and switched on the light. She was bone-weary, jet-lagged and totally depressed. In a few hours' time Margy would be bringing Val home but until then all she wanted to do was collapse into bed. But good manners dictated that she take care of her guest first.

'Follow me; I'll show you to your room. If——'

'Correction.' Justin caught her arm and spun her round to face him; his hard black eyes clashed with hers, a derisory anger in their depths.

'Our room, Zoë. You sleep with me. I told you last night, I'm not into celibacy—especially when I have a perfectly good wife at hand.'

'My, you have changed your tune. I seem to remember you always preferred separate bedrooms,' she was goaded into replying.

'At the time I thought it was for the best, but after last night I realised what a mistake I had made. Your fragile exterior cloaks a strong, sexy woman and I have no intention of making the same mistake again.'

She looked up at him, puzzled. She didn't understand his comment, but she was too tired to worry about it. 'Right at this moment all you have is an exhausted woman,' she said flatly.

Until now she had not really thought about what bringing Justin into her life would entail; she had not thought of much at all beyond wanting to save her child. Seeing his harshly determined face, she knew it would be pointless to argue.

Turning on her heel, she proceeded up the spindle-railed staircase to the landing and along to the main bedroom. She dropped her bag on the bed and crossed to the adjoining bathroom. 'Make yourself at home, why don't you?' she flung facetiously over her shoulder as she closed the bathroom door behind her.

'Mom, Mom, I missed you.'

'Yes, darling, and I love you,' she murmured sleepily,

and felt the warm touch of lips on her brow. Reassured, she drifted back to sleep.

Zoë blinked; she could vaguely hear voices whispering and the sound of childish laughter. She blinked again and opened her eyes. The small face was peering over the edge of the bed, and she smiled sleepily.

'Hello, darling; you're up early,' she murmured, and then she noticed his small hand curved in a much larger one. She glanced sideways, and slowly up long, jean-clad thighs, a plaid shirt, to the smiling face of her husband. She blushed scarlet and scrambled up into a sitting position, pulling the bedclothes with her, the events of last night flashing through her mind. 'Good morning, Justin,' she mumbled.

'Is it?' he queried, with a conspiratorial grin at Val. 'What do you think son?' And as Zoë watched they both burst out laughing.

'Nearly afternoon, Mom. Dad and I've been waiting ages for you to wake up. I've promised to take Dad to my favourite picnic place. Mrs B has got everything ready.'

'What? Oh!' Her startled gaze flashed from father to son and back to the man again. 'Give me five minutes,' she said, flustered by the insolent gleam of masculine appreciation in his dark eyes as they lingered on her small figure, and inexplicably angry at the ease with which Val called Justin Dad as though he had known him all his life.

She glanced at their joined hands and a shaft of pained jealousy arrowed through her.

'Come on, son. Let's leave your Mum to drink her coffee and dress in peace.'

'Not until I've had a cuddle,' Zoë insisted, her gaze resting lovingly on Val's face. 'I've missed you, darling,' she murmured, leaning forward and wrapping her arms around his thin little body. She buried her face in his sweet-smelling hair. He clung for a moment and then began to wriggle free.

'I'm glad you're home, Mom, but hurry up.'

It was fifteen minutes later before, with hesitant steps, she descended the stairs and pushed open the door into the large family-room. Justin was sitting on the battered old hide sofa with Val curled up on his lap, his small face a picture of rapt concentration as Justin's deep voice was describing what the Tower of London looked like.

'When can I go, Dad?

'As soon as you're a hundred per cent——'

'Hey, what happened to our picnic?' Zoë cut in, and they both turned identical brown eyes up to hers and her heart squeezed with a hope and a longing so intense that she had to turn away. 'Race you to the car,' she said, and fled, with father and son a few steps behind her.

It was one of those perfect, early spring days; the sun shone with the first real warmth of the year, the trees were in bud, the grass, awakening from winter, was turning a richer green, and as Justin manoeuvred the Range Rover along the narrow, winding coast road, with Val strapped happily in the back, keeping up a constant flow of chatter, she felt a new sense of hope growing in her heart.

And the hope grew stronger and brighter with every hour that passed. They parked the car and, with Zoë leading the way, Justin swung Val up on his shoulders and followed her down the winding path through the pine forest to the sea.

'Isn't it great, Dad?' Val demanded, once more on his own two feet. 'I named it Pirates Cove and nobody else ever comes here.'

It was a lovely place; tall pine trees edged a narrow ribbon of sandy beach, caressed by the eternal touch of the mighty Atlantic Ocean. She breathed in the fresh, healthy air and glanced sideways at Justin. He looked magnificent, dressed in well-washed jeans and a heavy navy turtle-neck sweater that didn't quite cover the collar of his blue and red plaid shirt. But it was the expression on his tanned face that shook her.

His eyes gleamed with such tender love and care down on the excited, upturned face of his son that it bought tears to her eyes. Swallowing hard, she briskly set about unpacking the picnic basket. 'Run along, you two; I'll give you a call when it's ready,' she said brightly, spreading a blanket out over the short grass on the edge of the tree line.

'Do you want any help?' Justin asked, his hand resting lightly on her shoulder for a second.

The sensual warmth of his touch triggered an immediate response in her that flustered her completely, and she was reminded of the meek way she had crawled into bed with him last night and promptly fallen asleep in his arms.

She shrugged off his hand. 'No, no. You watch Val,' she said, and added curtly, 'Be careful. Don't let him tire himself out. He's not as strong as he looks.'

'I am capable of looking after my own son. I'm not the uncaring monster you obviously assume I am,' he responded cuttingly.

'Hey, are you cross with my mom?' a little voice piped up.

The two adults immediately turned to the small figure bundled up in a wool coat with a muffler round his neck, his little face serious.

'No, darling, of course not.' Zoë recovered first. 'It's just Daddy's funny English accent,' she placated the boy.

'When I'm grown might I talk funny like dad?'

'Not so much of the "funny".' Justin rumpled the small, dark head with an affectionate hand. 'Come on, son; it's time I taught you how to skim stones.'

It was like a day out of time for Zoë. With everything prepared she sat down on the blanket and watched the two most important men in her life. They were standing at the water's edge; every so often a husky male laugh mingled with childish chuckles floated back on the breeze. She clapped her hands in spontaneous applause when a stone actually did jump along the water, and when Val skipped back towards her she laughed out loud as an extra large wave splashed up Justin's back just as he turned to follow suit.

They feasted on chicken legs, peanut butter sandwiches—a favourite of Val's—and home-made chocolate cake, washed down with Coke and a flask of coffee for the adults.

'Here they come,' Val whispered, and dashed to where Justin was sitting, his legs splayed, and crawled between them, hugging one large knee. 'Watch dad.'

Zoë envied him his position and immediately blushed at the thought. Justin caught her eye and, reaching out, curled his fingers around her arm.

'Come on, you too, Mom,' he drawled huskily, and suddenly she was sitting pressed to his side, the three of them a perfect picture of a close family. They smiled in delight as another family—this time one of chipmunks—descended on the beach, cavorting in the fine sand. Val threw the nuts Mrs B always packed and soon the chipmunks were brave enough to come near and eat them.

'I don't believe it,' Justin murmured, his usually stern face softened into a boyish grin as he watched the cheeky animals.

All too soon it was time to leave. Zoë glanced at Val; he looked pale, his eyes heavy, and, with a few quick words to Justin, they were packed up and back at the car.

Carefully Justin lifted the little boy into the back seat and strapped him in while she slid into the front passenger seat. She glanced back over her shoulder worriedly. 'Are you feeling all right, my pet?'

Val's drowsy eyes opened wide. A beatific smile lighting his whole face, he said simply, 'That's gotta be the best day ever, Mom.'

Zoë swallowed the last of her wine and placed the glass down on the table beside her chair. She tucked her bare feet underneath her body, her eyes roaming around the room, looking anywhere except at Justin, lounging on the sofa opposite.

They had bathed and put Val to bed ages ago. Mrs B had gone after serving up a delicious dinner. Zoë had finished her coffee, drained the last of her wine, and was overwhelmingly aware of the fraught silence in the room.

'It's nice; I didn't think it was you, but after today I realise it is.'

She jerked up straighter in the comfortable armchair. 'What is?' she said, completely at a loss as to what he was talking about.

'The house—I like it. Mrs B showed me around this morning when you were still asleep.'

'Oh.' She looked around, seeing the place as a stranger would for the first time. The living-room was comfortable with softly cushioned chairs and one or two pieces of good Federal period furniture, actually made in nearby Portsmouth. She didn't buy a lot of antiques but when she did she liked the best.

'I imagined you living in something like Wayne's place at Malibu; obviously motherhood has changed you.'

'Not that much,' she said shortly, but she wasn't about to enlighten him about her relationship with Wayne, not with Jess in the background. Instead she flared defensively, 'The house was built in the eighteenth century and as soon as I saw it I fell in love with it.'

'So adamant,' he drawled. 'Hey, I approve.'

'Yes, well...' She trailed off. She was proud of her home. She had tastefully furnished the two main reception-rooms in Early American style. The family-room she kept minimally furnished for Val and herself to play in. The hall still retained the original panelling, with the added delight of some interesting carvings.

In the olden days the master mariners and craftsmen who had lived in the area had also turned their hand to interior design, and the same seaman who carved a figure-head on an old sailing boat had been just as likely to carve a staircase when on dry land.

Personally Zoë loved the fireplace in this room; it was a prime example of the work of a skilled carver, and, with the fire lit and the pretty Laura Ashley curtains and décor, the room was cosy and intimate.

Too intimate, she thought, her eyes sliding over Justin's long, lounging body. 'It's not that big—only four bedrooms,' she said quickly—anything to break the growing tension.

'We only need two,' he drawled mockingly. 'Though I think the smallest one will do as a study for me. I'll see about getting it set up tomorrow.'

'But will you be staying that long? I—I mean...' She stammered to a halt. How could she say, If you're not a match for Val you can go? It sounded so brutal.

'Let me make this perfectly clear, Zoë.' Justin straightened up, his deep brown eyes fastening on hers, anger in their depths. 'You came looking for me. You found me, and I'm back in your life to stay. You're my wife. Whatever the result of my screening—however long Val does or does not have—I will not divorce you, and after the other night when you couldn't wait to get into my bed...'

She felt the colour rush into her face at his reminder and flinched, tearing her gaze away from the sensual, knowing gleam in his eyes.

'You must have realised that in law it constitutes a reconciliation and we would have to be separated another few years before you could even think of divorcing me.'

'But what about your work, your career?' He couldn't really mean to give it all up and she certainly wasn't moving anywhere. She had a life, family, friends, a business.

Justin rose and strolled across to the fireplace, to lean one elbow casually against the mantelshelf. He turned slightly, his expression grimly serious as he started to speak.

'I can follow my career from virtually anywhere; to-morrow I will arrange for the installation of the right computers. I see no problem. As it happens I've just finished a particularly long case and I have a clear calender for the next month. I had intended taking a holiday.' He studied her from beneath his lids, the tension rising.

'But that's not really the issue, is it, Zoë?' In two lithe strides he was beside her, his hip propped casually on the arm of her chair.

'No?' She swallowed nervously. He was looming over her, dark and dangerous. She wriggled uncomfortably in her seat and slipped her feet to the floor. But his hand slid under the heavy fall of her hair and curved around the back of her neck.

'The issue is Val and you and me.' He tilted her head back so that he was staring down into her wide blue eyes. 'Today Val thought for a second I was shouting at you. It mustn't happen again; the child has more than enough hardship ahead of him without our adding to it. Agreed?'

'Yes, yes, of course, but——'

'No buts, Zoë. You've done a great job with Val; he's a lovely boy, and he deserves the best. By that I mean two apparently loving parents. When he walks into the bedroom in the morning it will be to find his mother and father. Together. Understand...? No arguments, no fighting. A truce, if you will.'

So that was where he was leading. Why not? she asked herself. There was no surety that Justin would be a match for Val, and she had not given up hope of another pregnancy. In all honesty, she loved the idea of having another child irrespective of any health gains. She had been an only child and as a consequence had often felt lonely. In fact, she could have two or three...

She was beginning to feel quite euphoric; at least this time around he was prepared to share a bed with her, which was odd, when she thought about it.

She glanced up at him consideringly, through the veil of her thick eyelashes. He was so vitally male and yet before in their brief marriage he had rationed out their lovemaking and she still did not completely understand why. He obviously had no such hang-ups now if the other night was anything to go by.

Who knew? Propinquity might do what Zoë could not do before; he might actually fall in love with her. Then she remembered Jess.

'But what about your girlfriend?'

'Forget the girlfriend. I have.' His dark head bent, his kiss drawing all the air from her body.

CHAPTER NINE

'FOR Val,' Zoë murmured in brief defiance, against his mouth.

Justin's hands slid down and under her arms, their warmth penetrating the smooth cotton of her sweatshirt, burning into her as he swung her up and into his arms.

'For Val, yes. But don't kid yourself, Zoë,' he taunted, carrying her up the stairs. 'You want me just as much as I want you. You always have; the last four years haven't dampened the fire.' His lips moved sensuously over hers as he slowly slid her to the ground. 'Only banked it down for a while.'

She looked away from the passion burning in his eyes, the masculine confidence of his claim infuriating her. She tried to push him away and then she realised that they were in the bathroom. A sudden feeling of *déjà vu* engulfed her. The trouble was that Justin was right. She did want him. Years ago she had fantasised about sharing a shower with him.

She heard him sigh as he brought her up against the hard length of his body and any thought of resistance vanished. Her arms lifted to grasp his broad shoulders; she tipped back her head, offering her mouth, and the sensual, seeking warmth of his sent arrows of quivering delight soaring through her. His hand slipped beneath her sweatshirt and curved over her breast, and she groaned in agonised pleasure.

'Take your clothes off,' he said urgently. Pulling her sweatshirt over her head, he stepped back and swiftly pulled off his sweater and shirt and shed his jeans.

In a flurry, she shook off the rest of her clothes then hesitated, awed by the magnificent splendour of Justin's hard, aroused body. She felt the pounding of her blood in her veins, and as if from a great distance she heard his deep, husky voice.

'Ah, Zoë. I have waited years to do this,' he murmured, and then he took her into his arms, naked flesh to naked flesh.

She was burning, her senses swimming; she clung to him, her small hands curving around his broad back. She was sailing through the air! She was soaking!

'Ahhh,' she cried, her blue eyes widening to their fullest extent as she gazed bemusedly up into Justin's laughing face.

'I've fantasised for years about sharing a shower with you, little one,' he growled, his lips roaming over her eyes, her cheeks, and finally finding her mouth, while the water pounded down on them.

Wonderingly she gave herself up to his magic touch; she trembled when he picked up the soap and massaged the creamy lather all over her breasts and lower to her thighs, her legs, and back. She cried out, her fingers slipping on his wet skin. For a second their eyes met, his black, powerful, predatory, hers wild and wanting, and then he was inside her.

'Zoë, Zoë, are you all right?' She opened her eyes to gaze dazedly into his darkly flushed face.

'Better than all right,' she murmured. 'As fantasies go that surpassed them all.'

Justin scooped her hard against his shuddering body. 'God! I thought you'd fainted.'

'Silly.' She smiled bewitchingly up at him. 'It was ecstasy; the little death, I think the French call it.'

'Whatever. It's bed for you.'

Zoë sat on the dockside bench, an indulgent smile on her face as she watched the man and boy standing at the edge discussing the relative merits of the historic small boats riding at anchor. They had spent a wonderful couple of hours exploring the Maine Maritime Museum in Bath. Val had been intrigued by the shipyard, the joiner's shop, the rope-making, fascinated by the lobster exhibit, and completely entranced by the model boats.

It was only four days since Justin's arrival in her son's life, and yet, seeing them standing together hand in hand, one could believe they had been together always. A tinge of sadness dimmed her smile; this day out was a treat because very shortly Val was due in the hospital in New York to start the chemotherapy.

Justin had seen the doctor on Monday. She chuckled at the memory. She had gone with him to the surgery in Portland and to her surprise and amusement the arrogant, all-powerful Justin had gone pale at the sight of his own blood. Still, it was all the more courageous of him to have offered to be a donor, given his horror of everything medical, she realised generously.

His blood sample had been sent on to the lab in New York and tomorrow they were going to New York to talk to Professor Barnet and, she hoped, get the result. Because four days later Val was due back in hospital ...

She closed her eyes briefly and sent up a silent prayer. Dear God, let it be a match.

'He'll be fine, Zoë. Stop worrying.' Justin joined her on the bench, his arm going comfortingly around her shoulder.

The past few days, living as man and wife, had been surprisingly easy for Zoë. No, not just easy. Locked in Justin's arms every night, for a while she forgot all her troubles and found comfort in his masculine strength.

But sometimes, like now, the worry for her son over-whelmed her.

She turned bleak eyes to his, but before she could comment Val was scrambling on to her knee. She looked into his beloved little face, which was so happy, and had an image of him a month from now, minus his gorgeous black curls, his face racked with pain and her heart clenched in anguish. She wanted to weep. But of course she didn't.

They ended the day with a very early dinner at a steak and seafood restaurant with a nautical atmosphere on Front Street in Bath. Justin, at Zoë's instigation, or-dered the fresh lobster.

'You can't visit this part of the world without trying the fresh fish it's renowned for,' she insisted with a happy grin.

'Who's visiting?' Justin drawled sardonically, effec-tively dampening her mood.

She must never forget, she told herself sternly as Justin manoeuvred the car along the road home, he might be a tower of strength in her fight for her son's health, and he was a brilliant lover, as the past few days had proved, but however much she wished it otherwise he did not love her...

She remained silent for the rest of the journey home, and when Justin stopped the car in the drive she climbed out, but instead of going inside she hugged Val and gave him a quick kiss, saying, 'Daddy will look after you for an hour or two. I need to go and see Aunty Margy.'

Not looking at Justin, she set off walking down the hill. She had to get away for a while. She needed some space, some time to think, but Justin seemed to fill her every waking moment.

He had completely taken over; his computers were in-stalled in one bedroom, he was installed in her bedroom, and everywhere he went in the house Val was with him.

She heard their voices, their laughter. She knew she was being stupidly jealous. Worse, not only was she jealous of Justin's rapport with Val, but she was jealous of her own son. Just once she would have liked Justin to look at her with the same fiercely tender love he lavished on Val.

Putting her red duffel coat tightly around her, she bent her head against the wind and walked into the village. A long talk to Margy might help, and in any case she was shamefully neglecting the business.

Half an hour and two cups of tea later, sitting in the studio at the back of Margy's cottage, Zoë felt relaxed enough to talk.

'He's an incredibly... not so much handsome as impressive-looking man,' Margy said, grinning. 'And certainly a three-timer. It's just a pity it wasn't you he was doing it with. But then the best are usually swine, because they know they can get away with it.'

Zoë had to laugh. 'It sounds awful when you say it out loud, but true none the less. I actually dragged him away from his latest girlfriend, you know.' The grin faded from her face. It wasn't amusing at all. It was tragic...

'What's wrong?' Margy asked.

'Nothing.' Zoë stood up. She hadn't told Margy her hidden agenda of getting Justin into bed—getting pregnant. So she could hardly tell her she was sleeping with him again, and totally humiliated by her inability to resist him. Idly she flicked through a pile of drawings for Thanksgiving. 'I should be helping you, Margy.'

'Don't worry, I can manage the business; you look after Val. And yourself. Don't let your ex bully you into anything you don't want to do.' Margy's concern was genuine but she spoilt it by adding, 'Mind you, good sex is hard to come by; you could send him down here.'

Zoë laughed. 'Down, girl.' Then she caught sight of the clock on the wall. 'Heavens! Is that the time?' It was almost seven, and, with a hasty goodnight, she left.

Margy was great at putting things in perspective, she mused as she walked briskly back up the hill, the few street-lamps casting an eerie glow in the twilight. Instead of resenting the sex she shared with Justin, she simply had to keep reminding herself that her priority was her son. She had to be hard and think of Justin and his sperm simply as possible donors. But with luck he might fall in love with her—an added bonus...

She stopped a few yards from the house; there was a strange car parked outside the front door. She wasn't expecting anyone. Her heart missed a beat. Val. No, she was panicking; she knew the doctor's car. It was probably one of the many electricians or computer men Justin had arranged, and, striding on up the steps, she pushed off her shoes on the porch and walked into the hall.

She slipped off her coat, and, brushing a few stray tendrils of hair from her eyes, she heard Val's laughter coming from the den. Silently she crossed the hall and pushed open the door. Val loved a surprise...

But it was Zoë who got the surprise; all the colour drained from her face as she took in the view before her. Justin was sprawled on the floor, Val balanced on his flat stomach, and draped over the old hide sofa, laughing down at him, was his girlfriend Jess.

Her immediate reaction was to storm into the room and throw the other woman out of her house, but as soon as the thought entered her mind she dismissed it. They had not seen her; they were too busy laughing. Quietly she stepped back into the hall and pulled the door to.

She had vowed to sacrifice anything to save her son, and the full enormity of what she had to do chilled her to the bone. She stood in the hall looking vacantly around her. She didn't cry. She couldn't; she had no more tears left.

Pride, self-respect meant nothing put against Val's life. Justin held all the cards; he might be Val's only chance, and if that meant she had to put up with his girlfriend in her home she had no choice.

A few moments earlier she had actually thought they had a chance as a family. Never in her worst nightmare had she envisaged Justin being so callous, so amoral as to invite his girlfriend to her home, especially as he had spent the last few nights in Zoë's bed.

She pushed open the door again and walked in. 'Hello, Val, darling.' She spoke to her son, and feigned surprise at seeing the woman on the sofa. 'Jess, isn't it? This is a surprise. What brings you here?' Justin had jumped to his feet and she flashed him a vitriolic glance. 'Or need I ask?'

'Zoë, I'm so sorry; I came as soon as Justin told me. If I can be of any help?'

'I'm sure Justin will be suitably grateful, but if you will excuse me it is well past Val's bedtime.'

Sweeping her son up into her arms, she glared at Jess over the top of his head. 'Justin can get you something to eat. We had an early dinner so I'm going to have an early night. It will give you and Justin time to catch up on everything, and he can show you out.' She spun on her heel . . .

'Zoë, wait,' Justin demanded, and, catching her arm, he said, 'You're not being very hospitable to Jess.'

'Sorry, but in case you've forgotten we have an early start in the morning.'

'No, I haven't forgotten and Jess has kindly offered to stay and look after Val for the day.'

'Stay here?' It was even worse than she had thought.

'Yes, where else?'

'Well, you know where the bedrooms are; you make her comfortable.' And, tearing herself away from his restraining hand, she quickly left the room with Val held sleepily in her arms.

She closed Val's bedroom door behind her, and carried him into his own little bathroom. He was too tired to be talkative; she washed him down, and pulled on his Bugs Bunny pyjamas, and carried him back into his room.

'Top or bottom?' She asked the same question she always asked and knew the answer.

'Top, Mom, and isn't Jess nice?'

'Yes, darling,' she agreed, lying through her teeth, as she lifted him up to the top bunk. Val had chosen the bunk beds himself last summer when he'd graduated from a cot. A local craftsman made them in pine, the ends lovingly decorated in small woodland animals. Zoë had thought at the time that although she was not going to have any more children they would be good when Val got older and had friends to stay.

Now she wasn't sure he would get much older, and in the past months had quite often slept in the bottom one herself. Tonight she intended to do just that.

'What story would you like, Val?' She rummaged through the dozens of story books on the matching pine desk. 'How about *Sinbad*?' She knew it was one of his favourites, but when she turned back to the bunk his eyes were closed and he was fast asleep. Leaning over him, she kissed his pale cheek, her heart full of love, and whispered the Lord's Prayer as she always did, adding a plea for his full recovery.

Tears hazing her eyes, she stripped off her own clothes and burrowed under the Daffy Duck coverlet on the bottom bunk. She closed her eyes. She did not want to think, but she could not close down her mind so easily. Last night she had slept in Justin's arms, and tonight he

would be sleeping—no, not sleeping but something!—
with the lovely Jess. In her, Zoë's, house.

Zoë had loved Justin once, and with his betrayal she
had grown to hate him. Then, a few days ago, she had
realised that she still loved him. But now she hated him
yet again. The saying went that hate was the other side
of love—one emotion but sometimes mistaken for the
other. But as she lay curled up in the small bunk, her
thoughts spinning like a windmill, she came to the con-
clusion that popular belief was wrong: it was possible
to live with love and hate. Two opposite emotions could
coexist in one person. Her hatred of Justin was real; she
despised what he was. But she did love him.

She lay staring at the blank timber above her, won-
dering what the couple downstairs were doing now, and
hating the images that her vivid imagination flashed in
her mind. It didn't matter, she told herself. Nothing
mattered but Val.

How long she lay there listening to the faint, reassuring sound of her son's breathing she had no idea,
but suddenly the door opened and Justin walked in.

'So this is where you're hiding. I might have guessed.'
He strolled across to the bunks, leant over and kissed
Val, and then sat down on the edge of the lower bunk,
bending his head to avoid banging it on the bar. 'Really,
Zoë, you are being very childish. Jess was hoping to get
to know you better.'

Her eyes, widening in horror, flew to his face. Incredibly he was deadly serious. She could not believe the
sheer audacity, the barefaced cheek, the nerve... 'I—
I——' She couldn't find the words. 'Oh, get out,' she
finally said, defeated.

'Not without you, Zoë. Now be sensible.' His head
bent lower and his lips sought hers.

'No,' she protested vehemently.

'Yes,' he drawled throatily, his hand sliding around her neck and lifting her face for his kiss.

'Let go of me and go. I want to stay here with Val tonight. Have you forgotten tomorrow is the day we...?'

Justin leant back, his hand falling from her neck. 'No, I haven't forgotten. How could I? It's my result we're talking about, Zoë, and I had thought we could comfort and support each other.'

'I need to stay here with Val.'

'And what of my needs?' he asked sardonically.

She could see the angry glitter in his dark eyes by the moonlight shining through the window, and for a second she thought she saw despair, but the moon drifted behind a cloud, plunging the room into darkness, and she dismissed the thought, saying bluntly, 'Go and see Jess; I'm sure she can help you.'

She watched him walk away, and suddenly she didn't want him to go. Surely it must have meant something that he had come to her first?

Leaping out of the bunk, she dashed to the door, in time to see him disappear into the one remaining spare room—Jess's. Well, what had she expected? she asked herself fatalistically, and with one last kiss for the sleeping child she crawled back in the bunk, pulling the cover up over her head.

The journey to New York the next morning was horrendous. Breakfast had been a silent affair. Stilted good mornings had been exchanged between the three adults. Zoë had given Val a quick kiss and a hug before getting into the car for the first leg of the journey.

She hated leaving Val with Jess. The only thing that had persuaded her had been the fact that she had arranged for Margy to pick Val up in a couple of hours, and she had finally found the spirit to tell the black-eyed witch to leave as soon as Margy arrived.

She glanced sideways at Justin as he drove the car through the early morning traffic. He was staring straight ahead, his expression dark and brooding, and he somehow looked so alone that she couldn't help it—she put her small hand on his muscular thigh. 'It will be all right, Justin; we have to think positive...' She needed to talk, perhaps to disguise her nerves, her own worst nightmare. 'I know you're frightened of blood, but don't worry, you'll be fine.'

'Me, worry?' He shot her an angry look. 'If anyone needs to worry it's you. You do realise that if I'm not a match you have, in the last few hours, completely alienated the only other person who can help?'

'What? What are you talking about?' she asked, completely lost.

'Stop playing the dumb innocent, Zoë. I cannot believe how nasty you were to Jess, and she is our last hope. You do realise that, don't you?' he demanded with icy sarcasm.

'Jess?' His girlfriend? A horrible black chasm opened in front of Zoë.

The car screeched into the airport car park, and Justin, without glancing at her, got out. 'Hurry; the plane is waiting.'

She had to run to keep up with him. 'Justin, wait.' But he chose not to hear and he did not even look at her until they were safely strapped into their seats on the plane.

'Some mother you turned out to be, allowing your personal prejudice to blight Val's chances.'

'Who exactly *is* Jess?' She ignored his biting comment and grabbed his hand, which was lying on the armrest between them. 'Tell me, Justin.'

'Don't be ridiculous; you know perfectly well she's my half-sister. She might have been unpleasant to you last weekend but she had her reasons, and as soon as I told her about Val she came over as quickly as she could to offer her help. Which for some perverse reason you refused.'

'Oh, my God!' Zoë clasped her hands to her head; she could not believe what she had done, what she had thought of Jess. 'But wait a minute.' She lifted her head, staring with haunted eyes up at Justin's dark, implacable face. 'You told me you only had a stepsister.'

'I did no such thing. Jess is my *half*-sister—we share the same father. Why else...?'

He stopped, his dark, piercing gaze scrutinising her white face. 'Wait a minute; you mean you thought Jess was my mistress? You actually thought I invited a girlfriend to share the house my wife and son call home?'

Hard fingers gripped her chin and turned her head to meet the searing fury of his glance. 'You actually believe I am so lacking in morality, so despicable that I would do something so low? My God! I knew you had a low opinion of me, but *that* low...'

'I—I...' She had no defence. He was right; it hadn't been Justin who had told her he had a stepsister.

A memory of the past flickered in her brain. She had been telling Uncle Bertie what a pity it was that Justin's sister could not come to the wedding, and Uncle Bertie had replied, 'Well, she's not really his sister. His mother died at birth and Justin's father married the girl's mother.' Zoë had automatically assumed that she was his stepsister.

'Enlighten me, Zoë. How do you suffer me to make love to you when it's quite obvious that you despise me?' His hand fell from her chin and he straightened in his seat. 'Stupid question. You love Val, I'll give you that. And if I were you I would start praying that the news today is good. Otherwise you'll be crawling on your belly to Jess.'

'Please, Justin, you have to believe me; I never realised Jess was your sister. If I had I would never have been so rude to her, and I don't despise you. It isn't like that.' It was pure jealousy she suffered from, she recognised, but before she could say so Justin stopped her.

'Cut the excuses, Zoë.' His mouth tightened into a grim line. 'We'll see Professor Barnet, and hopefully the news will be good. If not I will personally ask Jess to help. I'll do everything in my power for our son. But, as for the rest, I find it hard to accept a wife who will prostitute herself, however good the reason.'

She rushed into speech. 'But it wasn't—I meant it isn't... I never——'

'Forget it, Zoë.' Turning to the stewardess, he ordered coffee, adding, 'Anything for you, Zoë?'

'I'll have a cup of coffee,' she said impatiently. How could he be so cool and withdrawn when she was bursting with emotional questions? As soon as the stewardess took the order she began again. 'Justin, you don't understand...'

'Please, Zoë, we have a tense morning ahead of us. Leave it. And let's at least try to present a united front to Professor Barnet.'

She clutched Justin's hand as if it were a lifeline as they were ushered into the great man's room and sat side by side on two straight-backed chairs in front of the large oak desk.

'Well, Mr. Gifford, I must say I'm glad to see you.' Professor Barnet smiled from behind his desk. 'Zoë is a strong woman but she was badly in need of some support. And I'm happy to say all the signs are that you are going to be a perfect match for young Val.'

Zoë jumped up; she was laughing and crying at the same time, hugging Justin, hugging the Professor, hugging herself. Justin was a *match*.

'It's very gratifying, Mr Gifford, and your son is very lucky. There's no reason why he shouldn't eventually make a complete recovery.'

Recovery! The word was music to Zoë's soul as she collapsed back on the chair.

'I didn't want to distress Zoë unduly before, but his chances were extremely limited without the transplant. Oddly enough, statistically one is more likely to get a match from a male donor than a female.' Professor Barnet looked at Justin, a purely masculine smile lighting his keen blue eyes. 'We men are apparently still good for something in these feminist times.'

Zoë ignored the chauvinistic remark and turned back to Justin, her blue eyes swimming with tears of joy and gratitude. She naturally reached for his hand; he curved his own strong hand around hers and squeezed it gently.

'I told you it would be all right,' he said triumphantly, but the relief on his rugged features was plain to see.

'All thanks to you,' she murmured and, unable to contain her delight, their earlier argument on the way there forgotten, she leant forward and brushed her lips against his. For a second he tensed, and she thought he was going to push her away; instead he pulled her from her seat and into his arms, and kissed her—a kiss of fervent hope, a shattering release of tension, and, she prayed, the start of something new.

They were oblivious to the old man behind the desk, until a discreet cough brought them back to their senses.

Hastily Zoë slid back on to her seat, her face a rosy red. But Justin, with admirable self-control and efficiency, said, 'So where do we go from here, Professor Barnet?'

'At your age, after a kiss like that, I would have said bed.' He chuckled delightedly at his own joke and Zoë's rosy face turned scarlet but she could not help joining in the general laughter.

Half an hour later, when Professor Barnet escorted them out of his office, she felt like pinching herself. Val was going to be all right!

She clung to Justin's arm as they walked down the long hospital corridor, her eyes sparkling like jewels, her face more animated than it had been in months. 'I can't wait to tell Val. Do you think we should ring? Do you think we should celebrate?' She babbled on in a cloud of euphoria until suddenly Justin stopped dead.

'Zoë, calm down,' he commanded firmly, and, grasping her shoulders, he turned her around to face him. He stared down at her, his expression deadly serious. 'We will not ring Val and in any case he's far too young to understand. Apart from which there's still a long way to go before he's cured.'

His eyes held hers, and suddenly she realised that he was probably thinking of the operation he himself was going to have to have.

'Sorry.' As she said the word she realised exactly how much she owed this man, her husband. She lifted her hand to his square jaw. 'Justin, I really am sorry for everything.'

She should never have run out on him. With the worry over Val appeased she saw things clearly for the first time in ages. Janet Ord had married, according to Justin, after she had dried out. Had Zoë let gossip and the drunken rambling of a discarded girlfriend ruin her marriage?

Her fingers trembled on his chin, and for a moment she thought she glimpsed the familiar flicker of desire in his dark eyes, but it was gone as swiftly as his hands dropped from her shoulders.

'Forget it,' he said abruptly. 'Let's get home.'

Her hand fell to her side and quietly she walked along beside him, lost in thought. He had called the house at

Rowena Cove home. Surely that was a good sign? He must be coming to care for her.

But her relief at the good news for Val was overshadowed slightly by their argument over his sister and his enigmatic statement earlier—something about a wife who prostituted herself, however good the cause.

She shook her fair head slightly; she was seeing problems where there were none, she told herself firmly. All she needed to do was apologise to Jess and everything would be great.

With a new confidence in her step, she smiled broadly up at her husband. 'Home and bed,' she said cheekily.

'Certainly,' he grinned back, and her happiness was complete.

But five minutes later her confidence deflated like a burst balloon.

'Zoë Gifford. How are you? Happy now?'

Her head shot up and she was looking into the smiling eyes of Freda Lark. 'Yes, yes, I am.' She grinned and chanced a swift glance at Justin; he was standing smiling enquiringly down at the attractive doctor, and she had no choice but to introduce them.

'It's nice to meet you, Mr Gifford. I was quite worried about your wife for a while, but I heard your good news from Professor Barnet. I'm really happy for you both.' Still smiling, Dr. Lark turned to Zoë again.

'Mind you, after meeting your husband I can see my advice to get yourself pregnant as quickly as possible certainly wouldn't be any hardship for you.'

Zoë felt all the blood leave her face. What a disastrous coincidence, meeting Dr Lark. She felt Justin's eyes on her but she dared not look at him, sure that her face must have 'guilty' written all over it.

But Dr Lark had no such qualms, she realised with mounting anger as the other woman laughed flirtatiously up at Justin, and his answering grin was all male arrogance.

'I'll take that as a compliment,' he said suavely.

Zoë did not know how she got through the next few minutes; she cast a fearful, sidelong glance at him as he took her elbow and ushered her out of the hospital. The easy smile he had exhibited for Freda Lark had vanished and his handsome face was as black as thunder.

'Justin,' she said tentatively as they stood together at the roadside, 'I can explain.'

But with commendable ease he had flagged down a taxi. 'Get in and shut up,' he snarled.

What should have been the happiest journey of her life—she was going home with the best news in the world for her son—was fast becoming a nightmare. Justin didn't speak to her; his face was rigid; she could sense the anger coming off him in great waves, and it was only when they picked up her car at Brunswick that he deigned to look at her.

He swung round in the driving seat, his face murderous, his black eyes boring into her. 'At last we're alone.' He watched her for a long moment. 'My God, I was so wrong about you. I thought you were a fragile young woman in need of protecting, when in actual fact you're as tough as steel.'

Zoë bit her lip. 'I can explain,' she repeated quietly.

'"Explain"!' he roared. 'What kind of fool do you take me for? Last Friday night wasn't about softening me up to confess we had a son; it was all about getting yourself pregnant. Yet again without telling me.' He slammed his hand down on the wheel. 'Damn it, I asked if you were protected, you little liar.'

She had no excuse. 'I'm sorry,' she apologised miserably. She looked up at his angry face. 'But I was desperate; I thought...'

'You thought you would use me as a stud—that's what these last few nights were all about.' A harsh laugh escaped him. 'Tell me, Zoë, who did you imagine I was when you went wild in my arms? Wayne? Nigel? And God knows how many more.'

Turning back in his seat, he stared fixedly at his hands on the wheel of the car. 'A bloody sperm bank.' He swore violently. Then his gaze flashed back to hers, black and pitiless. 'Right time of the month, was it?' he demanded silkily.

Her face burned scarlet and she had nothing to say. She saw a muscle jerking wildly in the side of his face, but his lips curled cynically. 'Last night? Ovulation over, so back to the single bunk, hmm?'

She swallowed hard. 'It wasn't like that,' she whispered, but her response was lost in the roar of the engine. She glanced fearfully at Justin and without taking his eyes from the road he shook his black head.

'I'll stay long enough to see that Val is OK, and to discover if I'm to be a father unknowingly yet again. Obviously I'll want to keep in touch with my children, but I see no reason to delay any longer in giving you the divorce you requested.'

But she didn't want a divorce. She wanted Justin. But one look at the granite-hard countenance and and she knew now was not the time to tell him. Although she had started out determined to seduce him, and was guilty of what he had accused her of, as soon as he had touched her, kissed her, she had been lost to everything and had melted in his arms. She loved him...

Jess was waiting in the hall when they walked in. She took one look at their faces and said, 'Oh, no, I am sorry.'

'No need, Jess,' her brother responded, with a tight smile. 'I am a match. Val will be all right, and now, if you will excuse me, it has been a long day.'

CHAPTER TEN

ZOË watched his broad back as he walked up the stairs, tears in her eyes. Her son was almost saved but the euphoria she had felt in Professor Barnet's office had been replaced by a numbing certainty that Justin was lost to her forever.

'I don't believe this. What on earth have you done to my brother now?' Jess demanded harshly. 'He looks positively grim, when he should be celebrating.'

Zoë turned her tear-drenched eyes to the other woman and, mindful of who Jess was, said quietly, 'Can we talk? I owe you an apology, but if I don't sit down I think I might fall down.'

Five minutes later, seated on the sofa in front of the open fire, she glanced up at Jess, standing in the middle of the room, and she could not believe how blind she had been. Jess had the same eyes, the same hair—the resemblance to Justin had been there all the time if only she had not been blinded by jealousy and full of preconceived notions of Justin's penchant for large ladies.

'I never realised you were Justin's sister until today. I thought you were his girlfriend,' she confessed quietly.

'His girlfriend?' Jess exclaimed. 'You've got to be kidding; my brother has never looked at another woman in years. The day you ran off to the States with your lover you effectively emasculated the man. He was almost destroyed. Then you turned up in London again and crawled straight back into his bed. Now you're trying to tell me you slept with him thinking I was his girlfriend.

God! What kind of woman are you?' she asked derisively.

'A very mixed-up one,' Zoë muttered. 'I don't know where you got your information from but I never ran off with a lover. I loved Justin to distraction but I discovered he never loved me. That's why I left him.'

'You're mad!' Jess stared into her tear-stained face and something in the smaller woman's expression made her hesitate. 'You honestly believe what you're saying.'

'It's the truth.' Zoë closed her eyes briefly, reminded of the pain and disillusion of the past.

'Tell me,' Jess demanded, sitting down beside her on the couch. 'Give me your version.'

'Oh, all the signs were there.' Zoë sighed. 'I had hints that Justin's reason for marrying me wasn't love, but I dismissed them as idle gossip. Until the night of my twenty-first birthday.'

Once she started she could not stop; it was like a dam breaking, and for the next quarter of an hour she told Jess everything—the gossip of Mrs Blacket, Justin's withdrawal into work, the separate bedrooms, even his restraint in their intimacy, right up to the night of Janet Ord's revelations. Finally she described the fatal meeting with Justin in California where he had made it plain that he never wanted to see her again.

'Incredible as it seems, I believe you,' Jess said, with a shake of her dark head. 'How two intelligent people could make such a mess of their lives is mind-boggling.'

'Yes, well, I blame myself,' Zoë said, with a wry smile. 'I was young and easily hurt——'

'And my brother is a repressed fool,' Jess cut in. 'Listen, Zoë, I know Justin loves you. He told me all about you long before he married you. You were his one topic of conversation for years. He even joined your uncle's practice thinking it would enhance his prospects as a suitor.'

'But he always wanted to be a judge!'

'Rubbish, he thrived on international law, but he gave it up for you. He worshipped you, and being a closet romantic he worried himself witless about the age-gap between you.

'He told me about your eighteenth birthday, and how he had taken another woman to your party. He was being noble. He was convinced you had to have the chance of a career, to see something of the world, before tying you down.'

She wanted to believe Jess, but if it was true why had Justin been so restrained in the intimate side of their relationship? 'Why the separate bedrooms?' She did not realise she had voiced the question out loud.

'Perhaps I can guess,' Jess offered, casting a reflective glance at her pale, troubled face. 'What did Justin tell you about our parents?'

'Not much—simply that his mother died at his birth and his father married again. His stepmother died when he was in his teens, as did his father a few years later. He never talked about his family; that's why I had the idea he had a stepsister, nothing more. Until today,' she said drily.

'Typical!' Jess snorted, before continuing. 'Dad was a Spaniard who had settled in London as a young man. He met my mother in the restaurant he owned. She was a ballerina—tiny, exquisite, a bit like you but dark. Justin doted on her; she was the only mother he had ever known and when I came along five years later he was equally protective of me.

'We had a happy childhood. Our parents adored each other; they were always touching, loving. Every summer we went to our villa in Spain for the holidays. Justin was only fifteen when it happened—a scream in the night. He dashed to our parents' room to find my father standing naked by the bed, Mother dead of a heart attack. She died...' Jess hesitated '...during *the act*...'

'Oh, my God!' Zoë exclaimed.

'Exactly my reaction. But Justin was at a very impressionable age. Embarrassed by his parents' sexuality, he was horrified and disgusted, and blamed Father for Mother's death. I heard him raging at Dad that at his age he should have more control—he should be past such things.' The two women exchanged an ironic glance.

'The naïveté of youth,' Jess opined wryly, before continuing. 'Bertie Brown was Dad's lawyer and a family friend, and from then on Justin spent most of his free time with Bertie, supposedly because he was studying hard, but to me it was as if Justin deliberately squashed the Latin side of his temperament. When Dad died three years later Justin had never really forgiven him.'

'So what are you trying to say?' Zoë asked.

'I'm no psychiatrist, but I do know my brother. He had girlfriends over the years—not that many, but every one was an amazon of a woman until you.'

Zoë wriggled uncomfortably on the seat, a snatch of conversation coming back to her. Sara Blacket had insisted that Justin went for large ladies. Could there be anything in what Jess said?

'He wrote to me when he first met you when you were a child, and even then he was obsessed with you, convinced that you needed looking after—a tiny orphan with only an old man for company. When I finally arrived in London after the wedding, hoping to meet my new sister-in-law, I found Justin completely gutted because you had run away.

'He told me that he'd been ultra-careful not to frighten you, either in or out of bed. Until the night you said you were leaving him, and he lost control. At first he blamed himself, sure that he had terrified you the same way he did on your eighteenth birthday.'

'He told you about that?' Zoë asked incredulously, blushing at the memory. 'But I wasn't terrified—well, not of Justin, more of myself; the feelings he aroused in me were all too new,' she explained. 'How could he have thought he was at fault?'

'Quite easily,' Jess offered drily. 'You ran away to London and he barely saw you for two years. He thought he had made the same mistake again and that was why you ran out on the marriage.'

A comment from the terrible night of their argument slipped into Zoë's mind—Justin saying ironically, 'And I thought I was being considerate,' when she had taunted him with Janet's words about his sexual exploits. Could he have been telling the truth? Was Jess's almost too simple explanation the right one? If so she realised that she had made a mistake of mega, mega proportions.

Jess was still talking and she listened with mounting horror, and the growing conviction that Jess was right.

'Until, that is, he followed you to the airport the last day, saw you in the arms of your American friend and realised you had a lover, that you had betrayed him...'

'But I never...' Zoë cried.

'It's not much good telling *me* that. It's Justin you have to convince, though to be honest I was under the impression that the pair of you had sorted out your differences.

'He told me last Saturday in London all about the child. He was furious at your hiding Val from him, but I know my brother and I knew he had already forgiven you. You were sharing his bed again, and he was vibrant—fully alive for the first time in years. But if the look on his face tonight was anything to go by you've crushed him again.'

'No—deflated his ego maybe.' And in a few, succinct sentences Zoë explained her attempt to seduce Justin into making her pregnant and how he had discovered the truth. To her amazement Jess started to laugh.

'My God, what a pair.'

'Excuse me if I don't see the joke,' Zoë said sarcastically. 'The man I love is going to divorce me; that's not funny, it's tragic.'

'But don't you see? There is my beloved brother terrified of his own strength, determined to treat you gently, and there you are, a tiny woman, equally determined to get him into bed, never mind that you thought I was his live-in girlfriend.'

One dark brow arched elegantly. 'And look who won! It's hilarious; you're as strong as he is, if not more so. You make a great couple. Or you will if you ever get your act together.'

Jess's chuckle ended in a wide yawn. 'I'm going to bed. If you take my advice, Zoë, I suggest you set about seducing my brother yet again, simply for yourself.' And with that parting shot she got up and left the room.

For a long time Zoë stared sightlessly into the flames of the open fire, rehashing Jess's conversation in her mind. It made a lot of sense, and it explained a good deal of the past. If she believed her...

Standing up, she slowly walked upstairs. She hesitated outside Justin's door, then moved on to Val's room. She gazed down at the sleeping child, and said a silent prayer of thanks and hope for his well-being. She kissed his smooth brow, and headed for the bathroom.

Ten minutes later, showered, her only covering a fluffy white bathrobe belted loosely around her waist, and with her face scrubbed clean of make-up, her hair brushed to a silken silver sheen falling in soft waves down her back, she quietly closed her son's bedroom door, and tiptoed along the hall to her own room—the room she shared with Justin...

Her mind made up, she took a a deep breath and, squaring her slender shoulders, pushed open the door and walked in. A single lamp was burning on the bedside table, illuminating the figure reclining on the large bed.

'Justin?' she began unsteadily, her hands curled into fists to stop their trembling. He was propped up against the pillows, a book in his hand. He was bare-chested, the hand-crafted quilt draped across his thighs covering his essential maleness.

'Zoë.' She looked at his face and flinched at the look of cold anger in his dark eyes. 'Why are you here?' he demanded harshly, the hand holding the book lowering to the bed.

'This is my room,' she mumbled defensively.

'Possession is nine tenths of the law,' he drawled sarcastically, 'and last night you made it abundantly clear that you preferred to sleep with our son. If you imagine for a second that I will swap places with you and sleep in that bunk forget it.'

'No. I mean, I thought...' She was stumbling over her words, but he sounded so chillingly remote that she had no idea how to continue.

'Don't try to think. I've had quite enough of your machiavellian thoughts for one day,' he informed her hardly. 'Dr Lark saw to that.'

'That's what I wanted to talk about—I mean I didn't——' She could not find the words 'set out to seduce you'; after all, she had. How could she explain that within minutes of being in his arms again her only thought had been how much she'd missed and needed him?

'For heaven's sake! Get to bed; you look worn out.'

He lifted the book and resumed reading. She was dismissed... Her shoulders slumped and she half turned, and then she stopped. No, damn it! She would not

meekly bow out. Justin had said, 'Get to bed,' and that
was exactly what she was going to do.

Swinging on her heel, her blue eyes glittering with
rising excitement, she ran across to the bed. A tug of
the belt at her waist and a shrug saw her towelling robe
fall to the floor, and, catching the corner of the coverlet
in one hand, in a second she had jumped into the wide
bed.

'What the hell . . .' he roared. The book went flying
through the air and the quilt slid down to his lean hips
as he raised himself up against the headboard and stared
down at her with a look of incredulous amazement in
his dark eyes. 'What do you think you're doing?'

'You did say, "Get to bed," ' she said innocently and,
turning on her side, she deliberately placed her small
hand on his hard, flat stomach; she felt his muscles tense
and his hand dropped to grab her wrist.

'Don't be frightened, Justin,' she prompted sweetly,
mischief dancing in her eyes. For once she had surprised
him and she intended to make full use of the advantage.
'I won't hurt you.'

She felt him stiffen; his fingers on her wrist tightened
like a manacle and suddenly she was no longer in control.
She was flat on her back with Justin looming over her.

'I will never give you the chance again,' he said
harshly, flinging one long leg across her thighs, pinning
her to the bed, while his hands formed a cage at either
side of her head. 'I've promised you I'll try and save
our son. I've agreed to divorce you. Damn it, Zoë, what
else do you want from me?'

She stared up at the ruthless, dark face and the breath
caught at the back of her throat. His Latin temperament
had certainly broken through now, she thought, a sliver
of fear racing down her spine. But he looked tired as
well as angry. Dark shadows under his eyes were accen-

tuated by the tautness of the skin over his high cheekbones.

'Answer me, damn you.'

'Nothing else,' she whispered, and, dredging up her last vestige of courage, she added, 'In fact, I don't want a divorce either. I want to stay with you—in your bed, in your life.' She felt the blood pounding in her ears; the touch of his hard, hot naked body against hers was dangerously arousing.

He reared back and surveyed her through half-closed lids. 'Am I supposed to believe that?' he asked with dry cynicism, his narrowed gaze angling down over her breasts. She felt her nipples peak in instant response, and cursed her inability to remain calm around him.

'What exactly are you after now, I wonder?' he mused, and bent slowly towards her. Shockingly his tongue licked tantalisingly over one taut nipple, before he lifted his head and added silkily, 'Or shall I guess?'

'Only you,' she breathed.

'Funny, I seem to remember last night you couldn't get rid of me quick enough, and yet last Friday you couldn't crawl into my bed fast enough.' Taunting mockery glittered in his eyes. 'I was flattered until today, when I discovered you were simply using me as a stud.'

'I'm sorry, I should have told you the truth—trusted you to do the right thing,' she freely admitted, but he was not placated.

'Yes, damn it! Yes, you should.' He swore in another flash of anger, his dark eyes burning down into hers. But as she gazed helplessly up at him, expecting the worst, he took a deep, indrawn breath, his mouth tightened and he was once more in control.

'I've had time to think about it and in fairness I can't condemn you for using me; I don't like it, but you had the best reason in the world—Val.' He moved his leg slowly, tantalisingly up her thigh, still holding her gaze.

'But now, tonight, you say you want me. Odd, this, from a wife who ran off with another man. For a wife I haven't seen for years. For a wife who forced herself to sleep with me for the sake of a child.'

There was derision in his face as his hard eyes swept down over her, inspecting her nakedness as she lay beneath him, then back to her wide, luminous blue eyes. 'I'm not a complete idiot, Zoë. Come on, tell me. Why?'

His distrust was only to be expected, she thought. God knew, she had shown little enough trust in him during their brief marriage; a bit of bitchy gossip and the drunken ravings of an ex-girlfriend and she had taken flight. She had no intention of making the same mistake again. But where to start? The beginning, perhaps. It meant baring her soul, leaving herself open to his ridicule, but she was going to try.

'Because I love you; I've always loved you,' she said bravely, reaching up to lay her hand on his broad chest. He looked very big, very remote, but she felt the heavy thump of his heart beneath her fingertips, and noted a betraying flicker of his long eyelashes; it gave her hope and then he smiled, and a frisson of fear darted up her spine.

'And I am supposed to believe you, and clasp you to my manly chest? Is that why you're here?'

The mockery in his deep voice was evident, but she refused to be cowed by it. 'No, I don't expect you to believe me, but I fully intend to convince you eventually,' she said boldly, hiding her fear. 'You're a very large man, very strong—to some people your power might be intimidating, but it never was to me.'

Her face was sombre, her voice low. 'I remember the first time we met and you held me on your lap and dried my tears. You were my gentle giant, and I had a terrible crush on you. By my eighteenth birthday party, the crush had changed to love, and I wanted you so badly.'

He sent her a sharp glance, and smiled without humour. 'Not that badly—you were terrified when I kissed you, touched you.'

She chuckled softly, gaining confidence, 'Oh, no, Justin; I wasn't frightened of you.' She allowed her fingers to curl in his chest hair. 'You were so sexy, my dreamboat. But I simply panicked; I was terrified by my own reaction; the feelings were so overwhelming that I couldn't handle them. But later, alone in bed, I ached and wished you were with me.'

'You don't have to lie,' he growled, the wariness in his expression giving her more hope. 'I know I came on too strong and you were disgusted.'

'I wasn't disgusted then, and I'm not lying now. I've always wanted you,' she husked provocatively, her sapphire eyes fixed on his. 'I want you now.'

A cruel, sensuous smile twisted his hard mouth. 'Yes, I can believe that. Four years on, and a few lovers later, you're hardly the shy, young thing I married.'

She flinched at his harsh words, but could not really blame him for thinking so badly of her. 'There was no other man, ever,' she said bluntly, willing him to believe her. 'The only difference between the last few nights we have spent together and the brief duration of our marriage is that now you treat me as a mature woman.

'Before you saw me as a child bride needing protection. I never did; all I needed was you, in my bed at night—all night.'

She saw the glitter in his eyes, and for a moment thought she was winning—until he stopped her wandering hand on his chest with his own much larger one.

'Why should I believe you? The girl I married would never have dared to try and seduce a man into bed as you did with me last week.' He held her hand hard against his heart while his other hand laced through her long hair, lifting her face up to his. He studied her pale features through narrowed eyes; only a nerve twitching in his jaw betrayed his tension.

'The man I married would not have let me,' she said flatly. 'You were always in control, always restrained. Did you really think, young as I was, I wouldn't recognise the fact?'

'And that bothered you?' he asked quickly, a dark flush spreading across his high cheekbones. 'You wanted more?'

'Yes,' she said simply. 'But I was too young and too in awe of you to tell you, and then after Uncle died you became even more withdrawn; you worked all hours, and didn't seem to need me at all. Then tonight Jess told me that you thought you were too old for me; that you tried to be noble.'

She knew she had to discuss everything, get it all out into the open, but it was hard. Justin had given her very little reason to hope.

Nevertheless, taking her courage in both hands, she told him everything Jess had said and ended with, 'I know how your mother died, and I thought perhaps it wasn't simply that you didn't love me but maybe because you were trying to be considerate. I remembered you once said that.'

She was rambling on but did not seem able to stop; she was too frightened. What if she had made a mistake, and he didn't care for her?

'God damn you, Zoë! Why, oh, why did you not tell me this before?' His mouth ground down on hers and he kissed her as if he would devour her whole.

When she was finally allowed to breathe she gazed bemusedly up into his brilliant dark eyes.

'Have you any idea of the agony I went through, leaving you every night?' he groaned, easing her back into the bed, his large body hard over her. 'Too terrified

to stay with you because I didn't trust myself to keep
my hands off you, again and again and again.'

Happiness, sharp and sweet, surged through her. It
was going to be all right. Justin slid his hand slowly
down, over her breast, the indentation of her waist and
lower, to linger on her slim thigh, and she moaned low
in her throat. His hard mouth closed over hers in a
ruthless, masterful kiss, and her hands helplessly sought
his strong neck and tangled in his black hair.

He lifted his head, his mouth curving in a self-derisory
smile. 'God, Zoë! You were my muse, my idol from the
very first moment I saw you. You terrified me. I only
had to look at you to want you, and I knew that if I
touched you I'd be lost; you were, and are, everything
I ever wanted. I loved you, but I was terrified of losing
you. You were so young, so innocent, so tiny.'

'It wasn't because Uncle Bertie told you to marry me?'
She sighed, closing her eyes and searching with parted
lips for his mouth.

'No, Zoë.' He rolled off her and, propping himself up
on one elbow, stared down at her flushed, bemused face.
'First it had little or nothing to do with my mother. In
fact, some people might say it was a lovely way to go.'
He chuckled. 'But Bertie was involved.'

'You don't need to tell me.' She wasn't sure that she
wanted to know the whole truth.

'Hush, Zoë, I do. Jess was right in a way. I took Janet
to your eighteenth out of a misguided sense of nobility,
but one look at you in that mini nightgown and I was
a goner.

'I was sure I had frightened you away for good, and
I'm not proud of the fact but for the next few months
I did have a brief affair with Janet. It meant nothing
and was soon over. Eventually I confided in Bertie how
I felt about you and the fact that I thought I had lost
you forever. He told me not to be so negative.'

'So you did discuss me with Uncle Bertie,' she said warily.

'Exactly! And that was why, when you accused me of doing so, I couldn't deny it, but not for the reason you thought. Bertie was a shrewd old bird and advised me to wait a year or two, allow you to finish your studies and mature a little, and then try again with a little more restraint.'

'I see. I think.'

'He loved you deeply, Zoë—almost as much as I did—and I stupidly took his advice again later when we got engaged. It was his suggestion—the master suite. He thought if I took things slow and gentle, curbed my baser instincts...' He smiled wryly. 'Well, you know the rest. It backfired spectacularly.'

The refurbishment of the master suite had been her uncle's wedding present; she had forgotten that. 'And I thought you didn't care and you thought I was too young, too fragile...' She touched his strong face with one hand. 'And I allowed my insecurity and other idle gossip to chase me away from you,' she concluded sadly.

He stared, his face grim. 'Are you sure that was all that sent you running? Not the handsome Texan, your secret valentine?'

'I always thought you sent the cards. You pretended you had sent the last one,' she said, with a grin that quickly vanished under his scowling frown.

'I followed you the last day; I saw you at the airport.'

'I swear it was pure coincidence that I met Wayne in the departure lounge.'

He caught her hand in his, his fingers tightening painfully around hers. 'And was it coincidence that you shared his house?' he said, with an edge of cruelty.

'Necessity.' She stared up into his strong, attractive face and willed him to believe her. 'I had to wait until he'd arranged my finances, and I had nowhere else to go; I was a whimpering wreck without you. But Wayne and I were never more than friends.'

Slowly the pressure on her hand relaxed, and he said deeply, 'I believe you, Zoë.' He kissed her long and tenderly. Picking her up in his arms and rolling on to his back, he held her close against his strong body. 'I have to.' He groaned as he kissed her again with aching sweetness. 'I love you.'

She wanted him to make love to her, but she wanted him really to believe her, and, forcing herself to lift her head, she leant back, her hands splayed across his muscular chest.

'And I love you.' She gazed down, her eyes wide and pleading on his handsome face. 'And I only allowed you to think Wayne was my lover because when you arrived in California you were so cold.' She shuddered with remembered pain. 'So remote, and you never wanted to see me again.'

'I lied; I came to fetch you home, but when I saw you in that man's home, looking so sleek and content, I was so hurt, so angry that I could barely speak. I had to get away.'

'But you refused to divorce me.'

He tensed suddenly, and looked at her with hard eyes. 'I love you, I would do anything for you, but I'm not the kind of generous soul who would hand over the love of his life to another man.'

She studied him from beneath lowered lashes. 'Then why tonight did you say I could have a divorce?'

'Because the male ego is a fragile thing and you severely dented mine and I was furious.' He laughed and kissed her mouth. 'But by the time I got up here I'd calmed down.

'It wasn't so much the fact that you'd seduced me into bed to get yourself pregnant.' His black eyes lit up with amusement; he chuckled again. 'Actually I had the same idea that night, and I was as mad as hell when you told me you were protected.'

A wide smile curved Zoë's soft mouth, and, leaning forward, she bit his chin lightly. 'Devious devil; I did wonder who was seducing whom at the time.'

'Yes, well, what really hurt today was the realisation that even after the last few days when I thought we'd finally got it together——' his hand slid down over her buttocks, pressing her into his hard thighs '—certainly in bed,' he said thickly, capturing her mouth for a quick, hard kiss, 'you still didn't trust me enough to tell me the whole truth regarding Val.

'If you'd simply told me another child might be another chance for our son... Instead I had to hear it from a doctor—a total stranger. If there's no trust between us, we have nothing,' he said with blunt conviction.

'I'm sorry.' She sighed. She'd thought love was enough, but suddenly she saw that it would never be enough, not for her and certainly not for Justin. She glanced at his handsome face and shivered at his bleak expression.

'I do trust you,' she said urgently. 'I was too afraid— the last few months with Val, the worry, the uncertainty; I wasn't thinking straight.'

She swallowed the lump that had formed in her throat, and struggled to contain her tears. 'I was going to tell you I was pregnant in California until you dismissed me so coldly. But deep down I always knew you would do anything to help. Why else do you think I kept your name and made it Val's? Why else would I have told him about his father?'

She could do no more; she had told him everything. She waited, heart pounding. His body wanted her—she could feel the hard weight of him beneath her—and she wasn't above using sex if that was what it took. 'I do love you,' she whispered, moving sensuously against him, her slender limbs twining with his.

He gave a hoarse groan. 'I believe you. As I said before, I have to. It would kill me to lose you again.' And then his mouth closed over hers with ravishing sweetness, the kiss so poignant, so tender that her eyes swam with tears.

'Justin,' she said hoarsely as she felt his strong hands move over her, tracing her spine, curving her buttocks, and swiftly their positions were reversed.

His deep voice whispered husky words of love and need and explicit intent as he shaped her to his passion. Then his hard mouth found hers again, his hands cupped her breast, his fingers teasingly tormenting on the taut peaks, and his mouth slid slowly from her lips to her throat and lower until her body writhed in wild desire.

She gloried in his impassioned, guttural moan when her small hands explored his massive, hard, muscled body; she nipped his shoulder with small teeth in a paroxysm of delight when he finally slid between her trembling thighs, filling her with almost unbearable ecstasy.

Consumed by a wild, raw passion, he lifted her bodily from the bed and she clung to him with legs and hands and teeth, buffeted by the force of his possession. They rolled around the huge bed in a delirious frenzy of passion.

She saw his dark head rear back; his features were cast in stone, rigid with desire, then his muscular body moved with savage ferocity, his weight forcing her deeper into the bed. His dark eyes blazed with primeval need, and she revelled in his total loss of control until she cried his name, her body convulsing in endless, great, surging waves of earth-shattering pleasure.

Justin stiffened. Head thrown back, he grated her name, then his big body, finding its release, sank against her in a long, frenzied moment of soul-shaking oblivion.

Later, when she lay beneath him, aware of the weight of him and the hot dampness of their sweat-slicked bodies, she lifted her hand and swept a curl of black hair away from the beads of perspiration running down his proud forehead. 'I love you,' she whispered, exhausted but filled with a wondrous peace. She had her husband back, her marriage back.

'And I love you.' The truth was in his deep, dark eyes as he smiled down at her. 'I always will.'

'I know.' She smiled with sheer delight.

'Confident little seductress, aren't you?'

She laughed out loud. Then he kissed her gently and her blood began to pound all over gain.

Much, much later, entwined in each other's arms, they talked softly of their love, their son, their fears.

'Don't worry, Zoë, everything will be perfect. Take it easy,' Justin murmured, his mouth brushing tenderly against her ear.

'But will you? Take it easy, I mean.' She remembered the days after Bertie's death when he'd worked twelve to eighteen hours a day. 'When Bertie died you turned into a workaholic. Why?'

He gave her a twisted smile. 'Stubborn little thing, aren't you?' But she could see that he was hiding something.

'Are you going to tell me?'

'Darling.' He kissed the tip of her nose, his arms holding her closer. 'We've wasted so much time; let's forget the past, and go forward from here.'

Thinking clearly for the first time in hours, Zoë turned in his arms to look steadily into his beloved face. 'I know Jess said you joined Bertie's firm simply to enhance your prospects with me. Is that why you had to work so long? Because you didn't really like what you were doing?'

'I love my sister dearly.' Justin chuckled. 'But as an anthropologist she has a nasty habit of not simply examining cultures but also trying to analyse me.'

'Was she right?'

'Yes and no,' he drawled, amusement in his brown eyes. 'You see, when my father died——'

'Jess said you never forgave him.'

'Rubbish. Jess has obviously said far too much, and I can see that you're not going to rest and let my poor, worn-out old body get some sleep until you're satisfied.'

She curled sinuously against his naked flesh and felt his body stir. 'Not so old,' she teased.

'Stop that and listen,' he said, with a faint smile. 'I forgave my father long before he died. But after his death, when Bertie had sold the restaurant and wound up his estate, there wasn't a lot of cash. I was all for dropping out of university and getting a job. Jess was still at school and there was only enough money to finance her education.

'Bertie, bless him, insisted on helping out financially. He was very good to me all through law school; I paid him back every penny, but I still felt I owed him a debt of gratitude, and anyway I loved the old man. So later, when I was beginning to specialise in international law and he suggested I was wasting my talent and asked me to join his firm, I didn't like to disappoint him.'

'But...' Zoë's blue eyes showed her dismay.

Justin nuzzled her neck. 'And I might—I just might—have considered improving my chances with a certain stunning little blonde,' he teased, with a lazy smile. 'But to be serious. After Bertie died and the will was read——'

'You were upset he hadn't left you any money.'

'For God's sake, Zoë!' He tensed and looked at her with grim eyes. 'Let me finish. I never wanted his money, but I was surprised at how little he had actually left you.

I knew that tax would swallow up most of it, but it didn't matter to me in the least. I knew his dearest wish was that you and I should live at Black Gables and I earned more than enough for us to be able to continue doing so. But then you decided you wanted to sell the place.'

'Not really,' she said slowly, feeling slightly ashamed of her shallow younger self. 'I simply thought it would be an easy way to get to share your bedroom.'

Justin shot her a wicked, amused look. 'Rather a desperate measure, and I didn't realise that at the time.'

His expression grew serious. 'I could deny you nothing. But I could not bear to see you lose the house forever. So I worked all the hours I could—and then some—trying to make enough quick capital to buy the house, hoping that later in our marriage when the children arrived you might want to go back to the place.'

'You would have done that for me?' she said softly, shaking her head in disbelief at the depth of his generosity.

'I did.'

'What?'

Justin stared for a moment at her puzzled blue eyes, then laughed wryly, drawling, 'You never read the papers you signed that day at Malibu, did you? The same as you never touched the money I paid to your New York lawyer every month.'

'No,' she admitted.

His mouth curved. 'Don't ever change, darling.' He kissed her and said gruffly, 'I bought Black Gables and I've been waiting years for you to return. I had arranged for the month to be kept free so that I could come and look for you.'

Her heart stopped; she stared at him, her lips parted in an amazed O. 'You did that for...?'

'Yes,' he affirmed, with a long, lingering kiss, and once again only the muffled sighs and sounds of love enhanced the late night air.

Zoë was sitting strapped into a seat on Concorde, flying the Atlantic to England, almost a year to the day since she had last made the trip. To her disgust she was slightly plumper than last time, but the tiny bundle of white-haired, blue-eyed joy in her arms more than made up for it.

She glanced sideways, as did the man sitting beside her—her husband. He caught her glance and smiled, his dark eyes shining with love and contentment.

'Are you and Mary OK?'

'Of course.' She looked down into her daughter's chubby face, a secret smile dancing in her beautiful eyes.

Their daughter had been born on Christmas Day, and she had been all for calling her Holly. But Justin had flatly refused and insisted that the child have an ordinary name, so they had agreed on Mary. But only because Zoë had heard him, when he thought no one was around, telling 'Maria' in Spanish how much he loved her, and she knew from Jess that it had been their mother's name.

She leant back against the seat, a deep sigh of contentment escaping her.

'Tired, darling?' Justin asked in concern.

'No, simply happy,' she murmured, and he bent and brushed his lips across hers.

'Me too,' he said huskily.

She glanced past him to where her son sat straining at the belt around his waist in his excitement. The last year had been hard but the love they all shared had made life feel good.

The transplant had been a success; they were on their way to London with Professor Barnet's blessing. Val would still have to attend hospital every few months for a check-up, but, barring accidents, there was no longer any medical reason why he should not live a long and happy life.

Zoë smiled to herself. Always providing his father did not kill him first, she thought, as Justin answered Val's never-ending questions.

'How fast is it going, Dad? Do you know how much it weighs? How old is it? Will I see the Tower of London soon? You said I would...'

An hour later she sat in the back seat of the long, sleek Jaguar with Val beside her as Justin manoeuvred the car into the drive of Black Gables and pulled up at the entrance.

'Oh, boy!' Val exclaimed; he was out of the car before his father had properly opened the door. 'Is this the Tower of London, Dad?' he demanded, running around the car to stare up at the massive house.

Justin took the baby from Zoë's arms and held the small child steadily against his heart with one large hand, while with the other he helped her out of the car.

'Is it, Dad?'

The two adults smiled into each other's eyes. 'Welcome home, Zoë, darling,' Justin murmured, dropping a swift kiss on her softly parted lips.

'Dad, Dad, where is the rest of the city? Are you sure this is the Tower of London?'

Justin, with admirable restraint considering he had a baby in one arm and a four-year-old boy hanging on to the leg of his trousers, said feelingly, 'No, it is not, son; this is our home for the next few months. But if you're not very careful you could just find yourself spending Easter in the Bloody Tower.'

'Justin, really—you shouldn't swear in front of the children,' Zoë remonstrated.

'I am not swearing,' he averred, and, catching the amusement sparkling in her sapphire eyes, he added astutely, 'That is the popular name bestowed upon the place centuries ago by the unfortunate inmates who lost their heads.'

'Always the lawyer with the quick rebuttal,' Zoë mocked. Their eyes met and clung and together they laughed out loud...

Still laughing, they entered the old house that was full of memories, with the hope of generations more to be made...

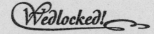

MILLION DOLLAR SWEEPSTAKES
AND EXTRA BONUS PRIZE DRAWING

BRIDE'S BAY RESORT

UNLOCK THE DOOR TO GREAT ROMANCE AT BRIDE'S BAY RESORT

Join Harlequin's new across-the-lines series, set in an exclusive hotel on an island off the coast of South Carolina.

Seven of your favorite authors will bring you exciting stories about fascinating heroes and heroines discovering love at Bride's Bay Resort.

Look for these fabulous stories coming to a store near you beginning in January 1996.

Harlequin American Romance #613 in January
Matchmaking Baby by Cathy Gillen Thacker

Harlequin Presents #1794 in February
Indiscretions by Robyn Donald

Harlequin Intrigue #362 in March
Love and Lies by Dawn Stewardson

Harlequin Romance #3404 in April
Make Believe Engagement by Day Leclaire

Harlequin Temptation #588 in May
Stranger in the Night by Roseanne Williams

Harlequin Superromance #695 in June
Married to a Stranger by Connie Bennett

Harlequin Historicals #324 in July
Dulcie's Gift by Ruth Langan

Visit Bride's Bay Resort each month wherever Harlequin books are sold.

HARLEQUIN®

BBAYG

A family feud...
A dangerous deception...
A secret love...

by Sara Wood

*An exciting trilogy from a
well-loved author...featuring romance,
revenge and secrets from the past.*

Join Suzanne, Tanya and Mariann—three very special
women—as they search for their destiny.

Coming next month:

**Book 3—*Threads of Destiny*
Harlequin Presents #1802**

László had appeared without warning...and Suzanne was
spellbound. But the potently attractive stranger had more
than romance on his mind.... László was out for *revenge*
with Suzanne as his target.

Harlequin Presents—you'll want to know what happens next!

Available in March wherever Harlequin books are sold.

You're About to Become a *Privileged Woman*

Reap the rewards of fabulous free gifts and benefits with proofs-of-purchase from Harlequin and Silhouette books

Pages & Privileges™

It's our way of thanking you for buying our books at your favorite retail stores.

Harlequin and Silhouette—
the most privileged readers in the world!

For more information about Harlequin and Silhouette's PAGES & PRIVILEGES program call the Pages & Privileges Benefits Desk: 1-503-794-2499

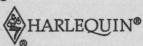

HARLEQUIN®